HAUNTING MUSES

GP *GusGus Press*
Bedazzled Ink Publishing Company • Fairfield, California

© 2016 Bedazzled Ink Publishing

All rights reserved. No part of this publication may be
reproduced or transmitted in any means,
electronic or mechanical, without permission in
writing from the publisher.

978-1-943837-52-6 paperback
978-1-943837-53-3 epub
978-1-943837-94-6 mobi

Cover Design
by
LJ DESIGNS

"In the Age of Resurrection: A Zombie Love Story." Copyright © 2016 by Deborah Walker. First published in *Zombonauts* (Library of Living Dead Press, 2009). Reprinted by permission of the author.
"Her gorgeous eyes." Copyright © 2016 by Giovanna Capone. First published in *In My Neighborhood: Poetry & Prose from an Italian-American* (Bedazzled Ink, 2014). Reprinted by permission of the author.
"Last night I was visited by the ancestors." Copyright © 2016 by Giovanna Capone. First published in *Curaggia: Writing by Women of Italian Descent*, edited by N. Ciatu, D. Dileo, and G. Micallef (Toronto: The Women's Press, 1998). Reprinted by permission of the author.
"Spirit Horse Ranch." Copyright © 2016 by Sacchi Green. First published in *Haunted Hearths & Sapphic Shades: Lesbian Ghost Stories*, edited by Catherine Lundhoff, (Lethe Press, 2008). Reprinted by permission of the author.
"Minghun." Copyright © 2016 by Amy Sisson. First published in *Strange Horizons*, 24 September 2007. Reprinted by permission of the author.
"They Come In Through the Walls." Copyright © 2016 by Bonnie Jo Stufflebeam. First published in *Expanded Horizons* (May 2012) and was translated into French for *Ténèbres* (June 2014). Reprinted by permission of the author.

GusGus Press
a division of
Bedazzled Ink Publishing, LLC
Fairfield, California
http://www.bedazzledink.com

For Mom: love never dies.

"Like a ghostly roll of drums remorselessly beat the measure of life."—Virginia Woolf, *To the Lighthouse*

Contents

FOREWORD ~ i ~ *Deborah Walker*

INTRODUCTION ~ iii ~ *Doreen Perrine*

DANCE WITH ME ~ 1 ~ *JL Merrow*

LABOR DAY WEEKEND ~ 6 ~ *Bonnie J. Morris*

IN THE AGE OF RESURRECTION ~ 22 ~ *Deborah Walker*

THE SUN RISES DIFFERENTLY ◊ HER GORGEOUS EYES ◊ LAST NIGHT I WAS VISITED BY THE ANCESTORS
~ 30 ~ *Giovanna Capone*

NEW HOPE ~ 36 ~ *Pascal Scott*

MY WIFE'S GHOST ~ 50 ~ *Andrea Lambert*

SPIRIT HORSE RANCH ~ 61 ~ *Sacchi Green*

MINGHUN ~ 79 ~ *Amy Sisson*

WINE AND MAGNOLIAS ~ 85 ~ *Lela E. Buis*

SCRATCH OF THE SPECTRE ~ 97 ~ *Lee Altomaro*

ENDURANCE ~ 103 ~ *Elaine Burnes*

LUCKY STRIKE ~ 120 ~ *L.K. Early*

BLACK HOLE ~ 137 ~ *Halee Kirkwood*

MEMORIES WICKED LITTLE GARDEN ~ 140 ~ *Jamie Sage Cotton*

THEY COME IN THROUGH THE WALLS ~ 143 ~ *Bonnie Jo Stufflebeam*

ANGEL OF LIGHT ~ 156 ~ *Doreen Perrine*

THE HAINT ON CRYIN BABY BRIDGE ~ 163 ~ *Xequina Ma. Berber*

Foreword

Ghosts come in many forms: visitations from lost spirits, and the ghosts of our past, memories for good and for bad. Death is not the only thing that can take from you, and hauntings can take unanticipated silhouettes. In *Haunting Muses* seventeen authors tell the story of female hauntings: stories, poems, and creative non-fiction considering what loss means to a life. Here are stories confirming our deepest understanding and stories to challenge what we know to be true. Stories familiar as our own lives and stories strange, poetic, and raw with real-life emotion.

Women have always written and published ghost stories. In the past, some stories were obscured. Lesbian themes and characters were half-shadowed: spinsters and maiden aunts, women on the outskirts of society, who could be coded for the knowledgeable reader. Writers, it's argued, sublimated gay themes into a more acceptable form in the transgressive genres such as horror fiction.

Things have changed. In *Haunting Muses*, lesbians are not confined to the shadows. The stories told reflect lives as diverse as real life, and those lives that are not always easy. The authors, be they award winners or newer voices, confidently explore the impact of loss on women's lives. *Haunting Muses* considers not only the traditional ghost, but charts the ghosts of loss: lost relationships ("Dance with Me" by JL Merrow) lost hopes, lost inspiration ("The sun rises differently" by Giovanna Capone). These are stories of ghosts real and metaphorical.

Here are stories that look to the past, present, and future. From Doreen Perrine's engaging historical tale of betrayal, "Angel of Light," to Elaine Burnes' exciting "Endurance," a story of danger, exploration, guilt, and reconciliation told under distant vistas.

The motif of the ghost is often a window into the past: in Bonnie J. Morris' "Labor Day Weekend" women from the past send a curveball into the present, and L.K. Early's "Lucky Strike" sees a young woman finding inspiration in the past to rise above her current troubles.

The past can also shine light upon current life: Giovanna Capone explores heritage in her poetry. And consideration of mental health is central to Andrea Lambert's moving "My Wife's Ghost." The changing form of child/parent relationship is examined Bonnie Jo StuffleBeam's excellent story, "They Come Through the Walls."

Some stories look beyond America's culture heritage. Pascal Scott's "New Hope" draws on Norse mythology. Amy Sisson's charming story "Minghun" is inspired by Chinese beliefs.

Yet American is not a monoculture. I was fascinated by the American lives described in Sacchi Green's "Spirit Horse Ranch," a story that manages to be both chilling and heartwarming, and by Lela E. Buis's psychic investigators Deep South story, "Wine and Magnolias."

These stories in *Haunting Muses* present a complexity of ideas that can be explored when we take one step to reality's left. These are wide-ranging stories, from the eerie to the uplifting. They show women engaging with the shades of the past, reaching for reconciliation and transformation. These stories show very different lives, yet all of one thing is constant, all lives encompass change, and loss is woven into the fabric experience. Here are stories about what is left behind after a loss, through change of circumstance or chance of heart: loss of a lover, loss of a friend, loss of a family member, even the loss of a stranger who has something to impart to us. These stories, poems, and creative non-fiction tell stories of hauntings good and bad, but always memorable.

Deborah Walker
London, 2016

Introduction

One way or another we all live with ghosts. Although I don't relish the idea of direct encounters, I've always had a fascination for ghosts. I am by no means alone. During my travels throughout the years, I've taken a number of ghost tours. New Orleans is among my favorite cities and also among the most haunted in the U.S. with ghost tours so large they get split into groups.

I was once joined on a ghost tour by a caustic ex-girlfriend who was nearly as scary—if not more so—than the spirits. During my only other vile experience of these tours a guide glamorized the human suffering behind hauntings in a manner that outmatched my fear of ghosts. (And, for the record, I fled the haunted jailhouse because of the guide and not the tormented spirits she described.) Let's face it—the living can be more terrifying than the dead.

Although grim and bloody tales drum up the requisite horror, I'm most drawn to messages that beckon from beyond. Writing ghost stories, hair-raising or not, also appeals as a form of catharsis for the haunted interactions that shape our mortal worlds. As I read the stories and poems in *Haunting Muses,* I was struck by how passion, more often love than hatred, causes a spirit to cross over from the other side. Like so many ghost storytellers and readers, I'm captivated by story, history, and by what drives a character to linger. And the ghosts of our lesbian lives and loves, be they remnants of the past or true tales of the paranormal, generate messages that must be told and heard.

Happily, Bedazzled Ink embraced my offbeat subject in this GusGus anthology, and its theme of literal and metaphorical ghosts generated a wealth of global submissions. Its exceptionality shines through the voices of established and emerging authors who deftly integrate the shadow world into their words.

The perceptive writing within these pages ranges from internalized slipstream, stream of consciousness, memoir, Gothic, to zombies and even sci-fi ghosts, historical fiction, and more traditional tales—all with a lesbian twist. I'm personally inspired that *Haunting Muses* features such unique glimpses into the afterlife, fused with insightful moments set within the here-and-now. Savor this anthology as a literary offering into which the otherworldly is interwoven through the rich and varied fabric of who we are.

Doreen Perrine
September 5, 2016

Dance With Me
JL Merrow

"READ TO ME," Helen says, perched up on the kitchen counter, her stockinged legs swinging. "Read some more of that book about the girl who faked her own death to frame her husband. I like that one."

"You would," I say. "But I can't. I'm cooking. See?" I hold up the knife I've been using to chop the courgette. It's larger than the one I'd usually use for vegetables, but it's beautifully curved and I like the way it feels in my hand. "Maybe after tea."

"You're soooo booooring," she moans, slouching in a parody of teenage ennui. Then she smiles and sits up straight again. "If you don't want to read, how about putting on some music? We could dance. You like dancing. I could teach you some more steps."

I look at the knife, its surface too dull to show my reflection. It *does* feel good in my hand . . .

I put it down firmly. It's only for a short while. "All right. But just a few dances."

Count Basie and Ella Fitzgerald fill the kitchen with swinging sounds, a little tinny from the small speakers of my iPod, and Helen shows me how to boogie forward. We did the boogie back already so now I can go both ways. Then she tries to teach me the jitterbug stroll and it's *so* complicated, you have to move your arms as well as your feet, and clap, and there's this bit where you have to crouch down. Helen makes it look so easy, but I'm all left feet. At the end I actually trip over myself and land on the kitchen lino and we just fall about laughing as Glenn Miller keeps on rollin' down the track to Tennessee.

I'm too tired to cook now, so I wrap the courgette up in cling film (if you don't look closely you can't even see it's been cut in two) and put it in the fridge. "Bedtime," I tell Helen firmly. "Coming?"

"What do *you* think?" she says, her smile wicked with promise, and we run up the stairs and fall on top of the duvet, still laughing.

I'M STIFF AND achy when I wake up. Comes of sleeping on the bed, not in it, I guess. Helen props herself on one elbow and looks at me with sultry eyes and bed hair, her silky nightie slipping off one tattooed, ivory shoulder. "Do you *have* to go to work?" she says with a pout so ridiculous I laugh and feel lighter than air, my aches forgotten.

"You know I do. How else are we going to feed your iTunes habit?" I haul myself up and peel off last night's clothes, all wrinkled and none too fresh. "I'm going to have a shower."

Helen's eyelashes shouldn't be real, they're so lush and dark as she looks up at me from under them. "I'll just have to find something to do by myself, then," she says, smoothing a hand down her silky front, over one breast and down, down to the junction of her legs. Her head falls back and she moans. "But I'll be soooo lonely."

I bite my lip. I can manage without a shower. It's only one more day.

I'VE ONLY BEEN in half an hour when Claire calls me into her office. She worries at a rough edge on her fingernail and looks at it, not me.

I'm glad she feels awkward.

I just want to die.

"If it was just the poor timekeeping," she says, and stops. "But it's been going on for weeks. And it's getting worse. I'm sorry, but I just can't have you serving customers in this state.

People have been talking, and we have an image to maintain. Why don't you take a few days off? Come back in on Monday, and we'll have another chat."

I trudge home knowing that everyone's looking at me. Teenage girls giggle on the bus, and all I can think is *me, me, they're laughing at me*. I feel a bit funny when I get off the bus, and I have to sit down in the shelter for a while. A bus stops, and the driver curses me when I don't get on.

When I get in the front door, though, Helen's all smiles. "You're back early! That's wonderful. Let's dance some more. Come on, put on the music."

"I can't, sweetheart. I'm sorry. I'm just too tired." It's like a knife in my heart, to disappoint her.

"But we have to do *something*. I know, we'll play charades. Come into the front room."

I follow her and turn on the standard lamp by the door. The curtains are closed already. I can't remember if I opened them this morning or not.

Helen looks lovely by lamplight. Her pale skin glows, and her eyes are darker than bitter chocolate. She's all leggy grace, dressed today in tight black trousers and an off-the-shoulder top. I don't know where she gets her clothes.

She's good at charades, too. I keep thinking I can trick her, but she knows all the latest films and shows. Books, now, sometimes I can stump her with a book, although I know it isn't fair.

But then, all's fair in love, isn't it?

I'm too tired to go up to bed afterwards, so we settle down on the sofa for the night.

I'M NOT SURE what day it is when the knock comes on the door.

"Don't go," Helen says, pouting at me from the armchair where she's curled up like a Siamese cat.

I nearly don't. But then the knock comes again, louder this time.

It seems familiar, somehow.

"I'll just see who it is," I say.

Helen stands up, her hands on her hips. "I *don't* want you to *go*."

I stare at her.

She's not so lovely, now. There's another knock, and I tear my gaze from her and go to the door, bruising my shoulder on the stair rail as I stumble past.

For a moment I think the door's locked, but then it opens under my hand, and I push it wide to see who's standing there.

It's Helen.

It's *Helen*.

She's in a new vintage fifties-style dress, skirt all puffed out with petticoats, and her hair up in a bun with two chopsticks. In her nose, she's wearing the ring I bought her, and told her it meant we were engaged.

Before she left me.

Her eyes are wide. "Sal?" she says. "Oh my God, look at you. What have you *done* to yourself?"

I look back into the hallway.

"Helen?" I say. My voice sounds funny.

Helen isn't in the hall, and when I run to the front room to look for her, she's not there either. I check the kitchen, and the downstairs loo, and then I scramble up stairs that tilt crazily, sick to my stomach.

Helen's not *anywhere*.

"Sal?" Helen's voice comes from downstairs. But it's not *her*.

"You made her go away," I shout, my voice thick. "You made her go away."

Helen-not-Helen holds me. "I'm sorry, babe. I didn't know. We'll make it better, 'kay? Come and sit down. I'll make a cup of tea, yeah?"

She opens the fridge, then shuts it again with a sound of disgust. "We can drink it black," she says, and rinses out the kettle, fills it, and sets it to boil.

HELEN SAYS SHE'S not coming back to me.

But we clean out the fridge together, throwing everything into a bin bag, even the squashy courgette in its clingfilm wrapper, and she makes me soup, bringing the kitchen to life with the aroma of parsnips, coriander, and cumin. It tastes so good, as if it's the first thing I've eaten in days.

I have a bath, not a shower, and I try to wash my hair, but it's so tangled I get fed up and crop half of it off. I think it suits me better anyway. I find some clean clothes and put them on, and throw the rest in the machine. After I've had another bowl of soup, Helen holds my hand while I call Claire at work and tell her I'm really sorry and I'll be in tomorrow.

But I still remember how good the knife felt in my hand, as if it was meant to be there, to be used by me. I don't think Helen really understands. Not *this* Helen.

There's a lot this Helen doesn't understand about me.

After she's gone, I dig a hole in autumn-soft earth and bury it in the garden.

Then I switch on my iPod, and let Ella Fitzgerald fill the house with warmth and sadness.

~

JL Merrow is that rare beast, an English person who refuses to drink tea. She writes across genres, with a preference for contemporary gay romance and mysteries, and is frequently accused of humour. Her novel *Slam!* won the 2013 Rainbow Award for Best LGBT Romantic Comedy, and her novel *Relief Valve* was a finalist in the mystery category of the 2015 EPIC Awards. Find JL Merrow online at: www.jlmerrow.com, on Twitter as @jlmerrow, and on Facebook at http://www.facebook.com/jl.merrow

Labor Day Weekend
Bonnie J. Morris

JUST BEFORE LABOR Day, the summer's morning air changed to sharp autumn gloss. That first feeling of the coming fall was a tang and a tentacle that curled delicately around every dyke professor in town. They all felt their antennae go up: school again. Both drugstores and bars proclaimed *Back to School Specials!*

Awaiting Hannah on campus were notices in her faculty mailbox: "The campus bookstore regrets to report that the textbook you ordered for Women's History 001 is out of print and unavailable for the fall semester." And so forth. The distance from freewheeling summer to sheer academic panic was a very fast crossing.

Should she give up asking her students to purchase real books and just go digital, with all her women's history assignments online, like other professors did nowadays? Why did it feel like such a betrayal to read Virginia Woolf on glass? Could there ever be a cyber equivalent word for *bookworm?*

But just below the fresh layer of anxiety, there was that glorious fire of recommitment, a feeling she recognized with gratitude and pleasure: her chosen work, examining the words of women's lives. In spite of the enormous workload, she still loved the cycle of the academic year, its curving arc of predictability ingrained since she was four and started nursery school. The weather obligingly shifted to cool; "kneesock weather," her mother used to say, meaning it was time to put away the shorts and bathing suits of summer play and pull on socks and saddle shoes for school. Hannah would beg and plead for just a few more days of running through the sprinkler, shirtless, free, unselfconscious, wearing her favorite pair of orange cutoffs, her threadbare PF Flyers tennis shoes. But school also meant books, when she was young and coming to realize how different she was from other little kids. Hannah's kickball-playing pals had hated library day, whereas Hannah found it heavenly. Now she was a grownup, and could read all day, every day, and not be considered a freak because it *was her job* to read. She had earned the freedom to be forever at home in history class, her mental pencilbox rattling, her heart and soul engaged.

BY SUNDAY OF Labor Day weekend Hannah was giddy with preparedness and back-to-school nostalgia, scuffing new loafers through a few early-turned and scattered leaves. She was on her way to Sappho's Bar for a last, lazy afternoon of watching baseball on the big screen Isabel had just installed, looking forward to sipping a brew with some of the big gals who were knowledgeable sports fanatics. Too soon, Labor Day weekend would be over and Hannah would be possessed by the demands of new students, by lectures to prepare, by hours spent with her nose in a textbook, deciphering the great women of history. Hannah took a long and winding route, walking to Sappho's instead of driving.

"Watch out, jerkface! You're going to hit that lady!"

Hannah jumped off the curb as a worn baseball banged her ankle. It rolled off her shoe, downhill into a side street; and two sheepish-looking little girls who had erred in a game of catch stood mortified but giggling in their front yard, awaiting Hannah's reaction. The bigger of the two girls, twisting her finger around beaded braids, ventured, "Are you okay?"

"I'm fine. You missed my soft parts." They doubled over with hilarity at that. Hannah approached the barefoot pair, hand extended to show she wasn't mad. "I'm actually on my way to watch a baseball game myself. I love to see girls practicing; keep it up! Either of you know how to pitch a curve ball?"

The bigger girl glanced at her companion, who was white and red-headed and wearing a backward-turned ball cap. "*She* thinks I can. My dad says I can't and never will. See, all we got at my school is slow-pitch softball. No baseball because there's no one to coach the girls."

"Well, there ought to be!" Hannah snarled, her feminist avatar uncoiling and rising like a cobra; and the girls involuntarily took a step back. "You know, there's a *law* that says girls can do any sport boys do. It's called—"

"Title IX," the redhead volunteered. "My mom's a lawyer."

Hannah looked at the sharp-featured little face, recognizing the dimples. "Your mom wouldn't be Elaine Grady, would she?"

"Ha, Susie's got *two* moms," the first girl said. "Now, how fair is that? I don't even have one. My mama died."

Susie frowned. "Shut up, Cubby. Yes, Elaine is my mom, but so is—"

"—Denise," finished Hannah. "Guess what: I know both of them. Okay. Susie, tell your mom Elaine to talk with Cubby's school principal, and I bet you can get a girls' baseball team started over there. It's been done before, you know? Grownup women played hard ball once. They were really good, too. In this league during World War II—"

"Yeah, *A League of Their Own*," Susie interrupted. "We watched that movie at my ninth birthday party in May."

"But it had just white girls," Cubby pointed out. "There was that one lady who could throw a curve and they wouldn't even let her into that ballpark."

The three of them stood there awkwardly, until Susie broke the silence. "Can you please go get our baseball for us? I think it rolled downhill behind you. We're not supposed to leave Cubby's front yard while her daddy's napping."

"Oh. Right." Hannah hurried after the lost ball, thinking: these kids know more than my own students. They don't need me to pitch lectures on women's history; they need female coaches who can pitch them curve balls. I'll have to get our athletic director at the university to shift money around and bring in a personal trainer for Cubby, ideally someone who knows the history of women in the Negro Leagues—but then she stopped cold, feeling her bruised ankle throb as her heart sped up. The ball had rolled all the way down the block and vanished into Willow Street. And Hannah had not turned the corner into that street in fourteen years.

She drove past it all the time, mentally chanting, *Don't look. Keep going.* Everyone had a street, she supposed, where the perfect love affair had played out, the architecture of a house and a street number containing the entire world of a finished relationship. In her own imagination it had never changed, that narrow townhouse, its yellow door opening right onto the old stone street, with a carriage lamp and a window box heavy with zinnias. Hannah had once loved a woman on Willow Street. She had loved the visiting scholar named Maud Nora.

It was right after Hannah finished her Ph.D., when she joined the university as a freshly minted young professor. They met over the wine and cheese at a reception for new faculty, talking about their heavy teaching loads and how to tackle it all, at different ages, different professional stages; Hannah with her new place in the world of women's history and Maud, older, better known, brought in for two years of special seminars on women's sports and culture. It was the busy, expert Maud who introduced Hannah to the history of the All American Girls' Baseball League. Maud even had an Aunt Marlene, nicknamed "Lumpy" for the bump on her head from a particularly rough game, who briefly played second base for the Grand Rapids Chicks.

And Maud—that had been a romance so all-consuming, Hannah barely remembered anything else about her first year of real employment. Yes, it was thrilling to stand at a lectern and watch students take notes, thrilling to take home a paycheck that soon turned into a leather jacket, a mountain bike, a complete set of Fiestaware, but most of that year was lost to kissing and waiting, kissing and waiting to kiss. With their equally demanding schedules, on some days they didn't see one another at all. On others—magic days, thought Hannah now—she was allowed to spend the night, leaving her grubby first apartment for the luxury of Maud's rented townhouse. They'd meet in that gold doorway, their leather satchels bumping. With a jingle of her keys, Maud would jab the door open and pour herself a glass of wine and settle on the couch with her half-glasses so charmingly askew, pretending to grade a few more student papers until the sexual tension wound up between them like a spring. Then Hannah had to pounce, to throw herself beseechingly into that waiting lap and bury her lips in Maud's cableknit sweater, the Celtic wool a fuzzbite in her teeth as Maud's own breathing quickened. On the sofa they made love while dusk began to gather, kids coming in from street games of baseball then, too, and cats yowling for their evening meal, and the train that rumbled every night at five. Eventually, on those special nights, Hannah would sigh and pull away and start a sauce for pasta in the narrow old kitchen with the butcher block island somehow fitting in between them, and Maud would watch the news while chopping vegetables or stripping husks off corn, and then by eight they'd eat their meal with jazz or blues or Bach—or women's music. Maud had every album ever made by any feminist musician, crates she'd brought with her from Ann Arbor along with a real stereo turntable and diamond-tipped needle; on such nights she'd raise her glass and say, "To my young scholar," toasting Hannah with one foot beneath the table stroking hers. That narrow house creaked and listed, groaned in autumn wind and froze them in the winter, so that Maud was often sick and Hannah always steaming her with pots of tea, with herbal decongestants, though Maud drew the line at "being vaporized," saying it sounded like a World War I attack. One night they both were bundled up in flannel, grading tests, and Hannah had her hair down and her bathrobe loosely tied, and looked up with the feeling Maud was watching, and she was. "Jesus Christ," said Maud, "you certainly are a beauty," and then laid her glasses down. They went to bed. But it didn't last. *It never does,* thought Hannah bitterly.

It didn't last because Maud merely went back to her tenured position in Ann Arbor, where she was closer to the archives and living survivors of the League, and while they travelled back and forth to see one another for a few months, eventually Maud made clear with firm regret that she was "done." Hannah had raged and puzzled and written bad poetry, trying to figure out what could have turned Maud away. The answer eventually proved to be a hunky umpire named Daniel, who was also interested in the history of women's sports. He, apparently, owned a complete set of original AAGBL trading cards and spent his weekends trolling flea markets for rare women's baseball memorabilia.

Left for a man. Left for a *man!* "Do you love *him,* or just his baseball card collection?" were Hannah's plaintive last words; it still hurt. The humiliation, on top of heartbreak, had ruined the very sight of the turnoff into Willow Street, which once excited her beyond description; she never again entered the street containing "their" house, not even when another faculty friend who lived farther down the block invited her to a holiday eggnog party. Maud's unexpected bisexuality was probably one reason why Hannah had eventually become involved with Gail, the butchest possible rebound partner; their first date lasted for so many happy years. But then Gail had walked out. Gail was gone, too.

Fuck it. Whatever. Hannah stepped into Willow Street, eyes focused on scooping up the children's lost ball, eyes blurry now with regret. Her hand shook as she touched the baseball. She wanted to touch Maud. She wanted to touch Gail. She wanted to go back in time and try again, forgive, apologize, be a better lover, anything at all. And as she turned at last to face the past, which was in this instance a townhouse at 307 Willow, another baseball came falling out of the sky and hit her on the head.

"IS SHE ALL right?"

"I don't know. *Marlene!* Can you get up?"

"Give her air. Come on, Gertie, shove over!"

Hannah opened an eye. For a moment she couldn't focus. Tense faces hovered over her—all topped with ballcaps. She recognized nobody. But she heard a cheer go up, and, for some reason, scattered applause. "Hot damn, she's okay! Atta girl. Come on, get back in the game! It's so close!" Hands reached to lift her to her feet.

"Something hit me," began Hannah and then gasped as she looked down at her bare legs. They were covered in bruises and scabs she hadn't had when she woke up that day. More distressingly, her legs seemed to be emerging from a skirt. A short uniform skirt. One she knew very well.

Hannah was a second basewoman for the Grand Rapids Chicks.

And that meant the year was 1945.

THE SUN WAS in the exact same position overhead, and the air had the same end-of-summer scent, but the women now pushing her toward second base had never known an iPad, e-mail, Skype, cell phone, even a television. Their chipped and crooked teeth, unrepaired by modern orthodontics, now smiled at her encouragingly. "Go on, we need you! Doreen's already out with a sprain. Can you play?"

"Can I play baseball? Hard ball? Not well," Hannah stammered.

"That's the stuff; if Marlene's joking again she can play. *Come on!* We still have a lead." Hannah found herself wobbling, on legs with unfamiliar sliding strawberries, toward a spot in a dirt field.

"Hurry up, princess," jeered an obvious dyke in a different color uniform skirt. "I didn't bean you that hard."

At the slur *princess,* which in Hannah's world had always been the unflattering term for a spoiled Jewish girl, Hannah forgot her dizziness and whirled around, eyes shooting cinders, teeth grinding.

She heard one of the players who had helped her up shout, "Yeah! There's that game face! Come on, now, Marlene!"

I'm not Marlene. I'm Hannah. Who's Marlene? A base hit snapped her to attention as dust flew and a sliding opponent landed with a thud on first.

"Son of an ITCH, that stung," the player moaned, and a shortstop from Hannah's team snorted in sympathy. "She can't risk another fine for swearing. The last swear cost her ten dollars, and a third gets her suspended from the League. That's Gloria—already busted for trying to go into one of those bars. Can't say as I blame her," she added, winking.

This is insane, Hannah thought, frantically fielding the next batter and missing the line drive by a country mile as the rival team advanced around the bases. *Marlene, Marlene, I know that name.* An ancient plane—to Hannah's eyes—sputtered over the field, dragging a banner that read, "WELL DONE TROOPS." *Wait!* Of course. Marlene was the name of Maud's aunt—the one who had actually played in the All American Girls' Baseball League. The one who got hit in the head at a game and carried a permanent lump on her temple that Maud had loved to pat as a little girl . . . Maud, who was much older than Hannah; who remembered and loved the League because she even went to a few games until her aunt finally retired in 1953.

What had Maud told Hannah about her aunt, during the days and nights they lived together? Hannah had worked very hard to repress those happy memories; but she sure needed them now. It was on that frosty January night when they made cinnamon popcorn, their hands plunging into a hot-buttered bowl, knuckles bumping, lips salty-sweet and slippery, kernels falling into their laps, and Hannah's eyes had been on their rented horror movie while Maud reminisced—what had she said, exactly, that night? "My aunt was probably a very gay lady, but they were barely allowed to talk about such things, let alone act on them . . . five-dollar first offenses were handed out for cursing, smoking, drinking, wearing hair in too butch a bob, getting off the travel bus without your skirt on, even just wearing slacks in a public place. Oh, my aunt hated those rules, but she needed to keep every nickel of her earnings to help out the family farm, which was still recovering from the whammo of the Depression years. Marlene could whistle through her teeth—she never got the gap fixed, the way most kids do now—and she had a special whistle for me, if she knew I was in the bleachers watching. She'd whistle twice during a lull in the action so I'd know she was thinking of me, and after the game we'd have Cracker Jacks together. Later on I recall that she usually had a woman friend with her, but of course when I was four, five, six, even twelve, I didn't put two and two together. After all, everyone on the team was a woman. And then they all had nicknames for each other, Slats, Mac, whatever; she was Lumpy, from being beaned with a ball, one game. She always said it was her piece of history."

Hannah tried to clear her throbbing head. The uniform ball cap at least shielded her eyes. She could clearly see the people in the stands, some in military uniforms, others in clean overalls or house dresses . . . just white people, too, she noticed, and certainly no one was texting or talking on a cell phone. No one had on headphones, ear buds, or Nike swooshes. There were plenty of kids, cheering and waving; mostly young girls—

And one of the little girls was Maud Nora.

DEFINITELY. IT WAS Maud, or rather a pint-sized incarnation of her scholarly ex, who on this last weekend of summer 1945 would have been about to enter first grade. She had on a short-sleeved sweater buttoned up the wrong way, a plaid skirt and Mary Janes. Her fair hair was pulled back with a yarn ribbon, and Cracker Jack glaze smeared her upper lip. She was screaming, "GO, Aunt Marlene, GO." Peanuts flew out of her mouth as she cheered.

Hannah parted her lips, afraid to say anything at all that might change the course of both their histories; and suddenly two quick and piercing whistles escaped from between her teeth. Mini-Maud shouted and waved at her. Hannah's head still throbbed from where she'd been knocked out—or, rather, knocked into the past and, apparently, into someone else's body; but when she reached up to touch her brow she was surprised to feel a cut and not a bump. *Hold on. If I'm "Lumpy," where's the lump? Or am I not Maud's aunt after all?*

"That's the game! We won! So long, Daisies!" shouted a player, and teammates from the Grand Rapids Chicks poured into the infield, whooping and cheering, while sullen Fort Wayne Daisies picked up their gloves and moved toward the waiting buses. In the bleachers, a little girl was waving, waiting. On legs that felt watery, yet real—there was no denying that she was alive and walking—Hannah approached young Maud.

The kid was five and a half. Not even a loose tooth yet. Probably couldn't read either. Her life was ahead of her: school, high school, college, graduate school, peace marches, feminism, coming out, scholarship on women's sports, tenure at Ann Arbor, a fling with a younger woman named Hannah, partnering with an umpire named Daniel with a good baseball card collection. There was no reason to approach such a tiny figure with resentment, or to horrify her by spilling the beans about a future she had yet to live. Hannah was mindful that anything she said or did now that deviated in any way from Maud Nora's precise recollections would change history, and probably wreak havoc with Hannah's own life somewhere out there—if she ever got back to it. She stood awkwardly on one leg, pulling her uniform bloomers down an inch, saying nothing.

"I saved you my Cracker Jack prize," babbled Maud. "I almost swallowed it. Then I didn't." It was a very tiny silver baseball glove. "Perfect for you, huh?" And she held it out.

Hannah took it from the sticky hand, thinking: this is a child; thinking: I am touching the hand that once held mine forty-five years later in time; thinking: how I loved that hand. Could she say to little Maud what grown-up Maud had meant to her? "I love you, pal," was what Hannah used to say in the dark; and that phrase came out easy now. And little Maud responded: "I love *you!* You're my *best!*" The very thing older Maud had told Hannah in the dark.

Maybe that was all she had ever hoped to hear again, one more time, because Hannah/Marlene's body flooded with nostalgia and she felt a grin crinkle all the way up to her cut forehead. In seconds, their meeting was over. A teammate pulled Hannah from the stands, saying, "Come on, we gotta *go,*" and little Maud was shouting, "I'll see ya, Aunt Marlene! I'll see ya! I'll see ya next game!" and out in the parking lot, safely hidden behind the idling team bus, Hannah sank to her knees in the soft dirt and wept.

THE NEXT THING she knew she was dozing on the bus, its leather seats, cracked and slippery, giving off a rank smell of linament, cheap perfume, hair spray, and stale Coca-Cola. Someone was whispering in her ear, "When we stop for dinner, we can try to find that bar I heard about. We got maybe an hour. I really want to get a drink, but we'll have to be super careful or there's hell to pay, you know. So are you with me? Are you in?"

Up ahead, a truck stop parking lot, half-filled with very old farm Fords and pickups, beckoned with lights spelling out "DON'S EATS" in sputtering aqua neon. Twenty tired, victorious Chicks tugged on clean uniform skirts and filed off the bus toward the diner, but Hannah's companion shouted, "I'll be back in a bit, I'm gonna take old Marlene to the restroom to touch up that bruise!" She guided Hannah toward the side of the parking lot, then hustled past the freestanding bathroom toward a street glistening with trolley tracks.

"Where are you taking me?" wailed Hannah, desperate to fall asleep and wake up back on her way to Sappho's, in her own time and in her own body; but her teammate had other plans. They passed houses with sagging porches, then crossed the tracks to an unpaved side street. Shapes of women and bawdy laughter drew them on toward one faintly lit brick house, its shades drawn.

"Just a bar, just a party Gina heard about," hissed her companion; and just as they reached the bottom step of the house, the front door opened and two beautifully dressed women reeled out. One had on a silk dress, pastel stockings well-seamed up the back, and a twisted pearl necklace. The other woman was in a pinstriped suit and sharp-brimmed fedora.

"Awesome," Hannah heard herself exclaim, before she remembered that was an expression very much from the future, marking her an alien. At the very same moment her seatmate from the bus yelled out, "Marlene, come back! Gina made a mistake! Goddamn it, that's a *colored* bar!"

The women on the porch were black.

"WHO YOU CALLING Goddamn colored?" said the butch in the fedora, casually but steadily taking the porch steps toward the rapidly receding Grand Rapids Chicks. "You too pretty to drink with us?" She looked at Hannah. "You two in that lily league? The white girls' ball league?"

The woman in the silk dress pointed a perfectly manicured middle finger at Hannah. "Pico's a better player than any of you. Think she could get on a League team? Uh uh. So why don't you go find some lily house party, and leave us our own spot?"

"It's so wrong," said Hannah.

The butch was in her face now. "What? You saying she's wrong?"

"No," said Hannah. "It's wrong that the League stayed white. I know all about that. I hate that about it. I wish it were a different story. I *know* how good you are."

The elegant femme gasped at this last remark, and Hannah realized how it sounded. Several other bar patrons had spilled out by now, and Hannah's teammate had completely disappeared, running noisily back to the truck stop. She was alone.

Fedora woman had not moved an inch away from Hannah's sweaty face. "You don't know me from Adam. You looking for a beat down, you come to the right place. You looking for a beer, your money's no good here. You looking for a woman, you not welcome."

All of a sudden, Hannah knew why she was there. "No beat down, no beer, no woman, unfortunately," she spoke as evenly as possible. "I'm just here for one hour, and now that's half gone. Me, I'm looking for your good curve ball, to pass along to girls who want to learn."

Gusts of laughter greeted this declaration, but the woman in the fedora narrowed her eyes. "You serious?"

"Pretty much," said Hannah, who had just realized who she was dealing with. "You're Pico Blue, aren't you? From the Negro League team. You got turned away from the all-white League and offered a spot playing with the Negro League men for one season when a couple of players were sent overseas. But the men won't let you pitch even though you have a better curve ball, because you're still a woman. I know about that. Well, I'm here to say I respect you. I tell kids about you. And I think I still have twenty minutes. Teach me everything you know."

Pico looked at her for a moment, considering, and then turned to her date. "Carlotta, get me my ballbag and glove. They're in the car."

"For real? We're supposed to be dancing!"

"Just do it," said Pico Blue, and Hannah thought: *there's a slogan someone waited to use in my time.*

They moved into the alley. Pico wound up, and Hannah was flat on her back in seconds, with the real lump on her head rising. *That's why she was called Lumpy! That's why she called it her piece of history! She couldn't tell anyone she'd gone to a dyke bar and practiced with black players. It was all forbidden; she would have been suspended! The AAGBL thought she got the lump on her head from that game against the Daisies!*

"Sorry," said Pico. "You got to shift sideways to catch me. Or didn't your friends tell you I'm a southpaw?" She wound up again, and Hannah, who had improvised a bat out of an old broom leaning against the house, managed to avoid being beaned yet again by chipping wildly at the pitch. The ball clunked up over their heads and landed in the gutter.

"Shit," said Pico. "I'm not climbing up there in this suit. You go up there and get me my ball. Ladder's just beyond that back window."

Hannah moved unsteadily along the house wall. Through the back window she could see women in butch-femme finery caressing, drinking beer, dancing to jazz, kissing in deep armchairs. Someone was serving up bowls of food from a big iron stewpot. Hearts and stars made from painted cardboard were strung across the bar, spelling out the names of a couple celebrating their anniversary. Ivy plants drooped from a high shelf. It looked startlingly like a night at Sappho's Bar—a place to go, to belong, to celebrate and kiss, eat comfort food and talk. This was the parallel world of segregation. This was separate and unequal, a site not written into the record of women's history . . . yet. W*e couldn't even go into each other's bars*, Hannah thought. But could anyone in the backroads of Grand Rapids in 1945 guess that thirty-one years into the future, the largest lesbian festival in the world would set up on a spot up less than two hours' drive from there? With black and white lesbians boldly out and proud onstage?

"Are you getting that ball?" shouted Pico. "I got a lady waiting on me."

Hannah could not take her eyes from the window. What was the name of this Michigan bar?

"Are you getting that ball?" the voice came again. And the voice grew higher. Then younger. "I got this lady waiting for me!"

STUPIDLY, HANNAH LOOKED at the baseball she was holding. It was Sunday afternoon on Willow Street. Two little girls, one black, one white, were standing in the front yard up the road and calling to her. Hannah felt her head: no bumps. Just her own springy Jewish hair. She was back in her own body, her own time!

She walked out of Willow Street, which would never again haunt her as it had. There were bigger ghosts to serve. "Here you go." She tossed the ball to Cubby. "But who's the lady waiting for you?"

"Miss Angie, my coach," the kid replied. "We've got practice up at school in an hour."

"For the new girls' baseball team," Susie explained. "Cubby's the pitcher! And coach is putting her in against the boys next weekend!"

"Miss Angie taught me a mean curve ball," Cubby admitted.

IF SHE EVER really needed a stiff drink at Sappho's, it was now. Hannah burst into the club just as Denise, Elaine, Vera, Mandy, and Jo were cheering the Yankees game. Bets had obviously been placed; Isabel was putting silver trays of snacks in front of everyone as they gathered under the new big-screen TV, and wads of cash shifted discreetly between trays.

"Elaine, Denise, I just met your kid," Hannah announced. "Nice little redhead. And her friend Cubby."

"Oh, Cubby's fantastic," Elaine confirmed. "We set her up with a personal trainer, Angela, the new athletic director just hired on campus. You know Angela's aunt once pitched in the Negro Leagues? Her nickname was Paco or Pico or something. Cubby's going to be just like her, maybe a pro someday!"

Hannah had put down a five dollar bill for a beer. Isabel

brought and uncapped the beer, then pushed some coins and a small bowl of Cracker Jack toward Hannah. It wasn't until she had taken four good swallows and removed her eyes from the TV screen that Hannah saw what was mixed in with her change: a tiny silver baseball glove, Maud Nora's Cracker Jack prize from 1945. She vaguely recalled it falling out of her uniform skirt pocket as she stood on tiptoe to peek into the window of the black lesbian bar in Grand Rapids . . . How had it ended up at Sappho's?

She looked at Isabel, who smiled back at her over the coins, and said quietly, "Yes; this is your change, the little change you asked for," and then went back to wiping down the bar.

~

Bonnie J. Morris is a women's studies professor and the author of fourteen books, including three Lambda Literary Awards and most recently *The Disappearing L: Erasure of Lesbian Spaces and Culture*. Her time travel novel *Sappho's Bar and Grill* will be published in 2017. When not teaching women's history for Georgetown University and George Washington, Dr. Morris is a consultant for Disney, an occasional lecturer for Olivia Cruises, and is working on a women's music archive for the Schlesinger Library at Radcliffe.

In the Age of Resurrection:
A Zombie Love Story
Deborah Walker

WHEN I BRUSHED my hair this morning, a few strands fell out and stuck to the hairbrush. They were adhered to a piece of skin and flesh around the size of an antique pound coin. I picked this coin of flesh off the hairbrush and held it to the light. I stared at it—as if I could see the fragmentation of my DNA in that small lump of tissue.

I threw it into the molecular bin at the side of the sink. Then I carefully brushed my hair to hide the already scabbing wound.

I stared into the bathroom mirror. That was that, then.

I would pod into the space-station today to visit a doctor. Then I would put my affairs in order: I would make two, long overdue visits, one to my brother Peter, and one to my darling Marla.

And after that . . .

"MS. PETROVITZ, I am sorry to inform you that you *have* entered the first stage of transformation."

The first stage. The point of no return. Stellar radiation had caused irrevocable damage within my body and within my mind. My DNA was on the long, slow escalator of deterioration. In a few weeks my mind would be gone but my body would live on.

There had been no real doubt in my mind, but I needed to have a doctor confirm the diagnosis.

"Have you entered it onto my medical records?" I asked.

"Yes, ma'am." The doctor's face was professional stone. I wondered how many times he had delivered this diagnosis.

"I can arrange a counselling session for you, and I can also recommend a very active self-help group."

"No thanks, Doctor. That's not my style." I stood up and held out my hand. "I intended to get euthanized and my chip activated as quickly as possible."

I had no intention of enduring the long, slow process of dissolution.

"Well, that's your choice, Ms. Petrovitz, but I would caution you against making any hasty decisions."

"Doctor, I knew what the score was when I came to this part of space. I made my decision a long time ago."

"As you wish."

A zombie was entering data into a processor at the front desk. They can be trained for simple tasks. It looked like a women, a small frame encased in a flexible silver metal-rub suit holding her body together. I gave her a wave as I left the doctor's office. There's no stigma here, as there is on Earth. We cherish our zombies. They're part of our life.

Why wouldn't we, when we know that we will become them?

I'VE WORKED AS a miner for the last ten years. I have my own asteroid and a snug living space carved out of the rock. Now that I had the official diagnosis, I hooked up to the net and willed my home and mining rights over to Cassidy Sung. That would give her a shock. Before I met Marla, me and Cass had an on-off relationship for years. You know the type of thing.

Still, I hoped that me passing on the asteroid to her would mean something to Cass. I didn't vid her, nothing much to say. Actions speak louder than words, in my opinion. I hoped she'd get some enjoyment out of the money my asteroid would bring her.

I was in a thoughtful mood as I walked the space station High Street along to the Church of the Resurrected Flesh. As I looked around the street I could see normals and zombies all mixed up together. We've built a fine place out here in this corner of space, we're tolerant here.

And I've seen things that the human eye was never built to see. I've seen the sun rise and set on a dozen worlds; I've marvelled at the slow dance of strange lights over the ruins of ancient worlds; I've met people, weird people who have blown my mind with their alien philosophies. I have no regrets.

"Sister."

The voice of a priest called out from a balcony on the Church. He was dressed in the garments of one of the resurrected, although he was a normal. He wouldn't be able to talk otherwise.

"It's later than you think. Come into the Church and prepare yourself."

That made me stop for a minute. He was looking at me like he could tell, but by my reckoning, I had a couple of weeks to go before my mind went. Perhaps the priests develop some sort of sense about these things.

"I'm coming in, anyway," I shouted.

"Hallelujah, Sister."

"I'm just here to see my brother," I said.

I was sorry to disappoint him. I've never been one to be into religion, much. I imagine it's a comfort to some. That flake of flesh this morning hadn't changed my perspective.

The priest on the balcony looked at me properly for the first time, seeing not a potential soul to be saved, but a person. "Ah, yes. You're Brother Peter's sister aren't you? Come in and be welcome. I saw him working in his cell half an hour ago."

I walked into the church and past the rows of pews that were filled with the resurrected. Their hands moved over church beads, as they made their prayers to God. Rich folk buy their contracts and set them here, saying prayers for their souls.

A light blinked at the back of each of the zombies' necks, the electronic pulse that bathed their damaged brains in hormones. That flash of light kept us safe, turned them into supplicants and stopped them from becoming what was their nature—flesh-eating, mindless creatures.

I walked to Peter's cell and knocked on the open door. "Hey, Peter."

My brother was dressed in a metal-rub suit, too, but he'd pushed down the face covering mask.

He was engrossed in his work, as usual. "Have you heard what the scientists are saying?"

He almost spat out the word "scientists." As if science wasn't the thing that bought us here and had gifted us with this spectacular life in the stars.

I peered over his shoulder trying to read the paper upside down. "What are they saying this time?" I asked.

"They say that they're on the verge of a cure for transformation." He jabbed his finger angrily at the article.

My heart beat wildly for a foolish moment.

A cure?

But reality quickly reasserted itself. If there was a cure—and that was doubtful—it was too late for me. I was already walking along the dark tunnel. I felt glad that someone was waiting at the end for me.

"There'll be no cure, Peter. They've been on the verge of cure for the last fifty years."

"There say that there's a new way of blocking out the stellar radiation." He stood up, walked to the window of his cell, and looked out on the rows of zombie supplicants in the nave. "As if we want a cure. Look at the supplicants out there. Everything that made them human is gone, they're brain-dead. Here in the heavens His rays delete the old self, but they live on. They're in a state of innocence. They are incapable of sin. Even though their bodies continue to degrade, the power of His love has bestowed a miraculous regeneration on the limbs."

I didn't say if it weren't for that pulse in the back of their necks, bathing the supplicants in calming hormones those innocents would be tearing us limb from limb. I didn't want to argue with him, not now. So I said, "It's a miracle alright."

He smiled at me. "Have you found the light, Pat?"

He was kidding. Peter knew that I didn't share his faith, that I thought the Church was just a crutch for those who couldn't accept the reality of living in space.

If you live here, radiation causes incremental damage to your DNA. Eventually you reach the transformation point, and your mind dies. What happens afterwards—the continuation of the body—didn't seem like a miracle to me. It was just a trick of biology. The same stellar radiation that killed your mind activated an older simpler part of the brain that allowed you to keep on moving. These multiple layers of our brains were just a consequence of our stroll through the long slow path of evolution.

"What's wrong, Pat?"

He was my brother—he knew me.

"I've got something to tell you, Peter."

He stopped reading the article and looked at me.

"My transformation's started."

"Oh, Pat." He reached out and took my hand. I could see that he was conflicted. As a priest, it was wonderful news, another soul was about to enter the resurrected afterlife, but as a brother the news was not so good.

"And have you changed your mind about the Church?"

"No, Peter, I'm sorry."

It crossed my mind that I should lie to him, just to make him happy. It would mean an awful lot to him. But that wouldn't have been right.

"What are you going to do?"

"I don't want to linger."

Some people hid their transformation, putting off the inevitable for as long as possible, but not me. I wanted to make my good-byes today. Tomorrow I would go to the bureau, and get the final dose of radiation.

"That's what I would have expected of you." We hugged. "You've had a good life, Pat."

"Will you promise me something, Peter?"

"Whatever you want."

"Promise me that you won't make me into a supplicant when I'm dead."

"Of course, not. I respect your wishes."

I breathed a sigh of relief, that was the thing I feared most.

Because when I'm dead, I wanted to spend the rest of my existence with my girl.

I WENT TO see my love.

I hadn't been to see her for a few weeks. You know how it is when somebody dies, at first you visit them every day, and then little by little the visits begin to diminish. You start to get on with your life again. But some things don't diminish, I missed her every day, every minute. She was still my lovely girl.

She worked in the hydroponics factory. She'd always loved growing things. The living space in my asteroid had born testimony to her obsession. I smiled. I only hoped that she was more successful here than she had been in our home. I was forever throwing out her dead ferns and whatnot.

I waited for her shift to finish, watching the silver suited zombies completing their simple tasks. Their unhurried, deliberate movements were replicated throughout the factory. They reminded me of a shoal of silver fish swimming through the ocean of their afterlife. They were . . . cohesive, I felt an inkling of what my brother had been trying to teach me all these years.

At the end of the shift they bought Marla to me and guided her to a chair.

"Marla, my love."

I took her hand and felt her skin through the silver of the suit. I stared into her eyes, looking for recognition but there was nothing there.

It's unknown how much the zombies remember. It's a matter of research or a matter of faith, depending on your point of view. The Church argues that zombies have entered a state of purity, that their minds are lodged in heaven, while their bodies fall back into the clay.

Others, those who don't understand, are less generous. They say that the zombies are automatons, or even monsters like the zombies of old, inhabited by malevolence.

They would not say that if they could look into the eyes of my love. I believe that she can hear me.

"It has been a long time, since you left me, Marla. I've been lonely without you. But I have good news. I will be joining you tomorrow."

I scan her eyes.

"You've gone ahead, but I'm expecting you to show me the ropes, just like you always did. You always looked out for me."

I'm crying now, willing for some reaction in her eyes.

But there is none.

It is too much for me. I do not want to linger. I leave her sitting in the chair. Looking forward to the morrow when I will enter the bureau.

I will complete the process that started when I first came here. They will bathe my head in radiation, my mind will slip away, my relentless brain will stop. The chip on the back of my neck will activate and I will step into the underworld.

Where I will be with my love, Marla, as I was in life, so I will be in death.

Deborah Walker grew up in the most English town in the country, but she soon hightailed it down to London, where she now lives with her partner, Chris, and her two teenage children. Find Deborah in the British Museum trawling the past for future inspiration or on her blog: http://deborahwalkersbibliography.blogspot.co.uk/. Her stories have appeared in *Fantastic Stories of the Imagination, Nature's Futures, Lady Churchill's Rosebud Wristlet* and *The Year's Best SF 18* and have been translated into over a dozen languages.

Poems
Giovanna Capone

The sun rises differently

and the moon doesn't shine
Sunsets don't expand like lavender mist
seeping across the lake

this lake we circled together
so many times

But tonight nothing's right
there's no lightness in my step
and even the crickets forget
to sing their songs

Instead the lake is quiet
and the sky a dull gray
capping off an uneventful day
with no word or text from you

The sun rises differently
and my mornings are infinitely less
prone to beauty or joy

and every decoy I use
to distract or self-soothe
is not working

Sadness is lurking
just a step away.

Her gorgeous eyes

stare at me
from a computer screen

The headlines scream
Amy Winehouse, dead at 27
Black eye liner and full make-up
tattooed shoulders and behive,
she had soul beyond her years

My tears won't stop,
I go home and flop on the bed
slapping the wall
remembering her cockney drawl

On youtube the journalist was seeking the perfect question
What more to know?
Her life was an open wound
infected and sore
for all to see

Her lyrics describing to a T
the agony of an ex
the mess of a reckless affair
She was Ella and Billie and Janis
A moon shining in the dark

The voice that put it so stark
soldering her pain
to vintage music

Last night I was visited by the ancestors

They sat heavy in my dreams
the dead ones
now undead
were talking, laughing
resting their hands on big bellies.
There was coffee
in demitasse cups
and Entenmann's crumb cake
on the table,
a cardboard box of cannoli
and almond biscotti from Artuso's Bakery
and lots of loud laughter
"Ha ha ha!
She thinks she's different from us
because she's queer?"

"Non farmi ridere!"* one aunt said.
"Same problems, same pain.
Same old shit!"
Then the others burst out laughing
and they all laughed long and hard.
They seemed to have a consensus on me
and on life in general
which is that it's useless
to try too hard
to be happy
"Hey, you get what you get and that's it
Stop crying the blues."

Va fanculo!
These ancestors
you sit too heavy in my dreams
as you do in my waking life
where at times
your immigrant resignation
feels like a quicksand
I sink into
a mud, so deep and familiar
I could make my home in it
—and suffocate
Big hands resting on round bellies, thick fingers
and brown fleshy arms,
Your gray black hair is done up perfect
a dark red color
highlights your lips
Big gray dresses
hang past your knees
You speak in loud, deep voices, wave your hands around
and keep a few small, slender men by your side
men like my father
who actually seem kinder
than you goddamn women
Madonna!
with your volcanic laughter
You all sit in judgment
on me
Loud voices dominate
laughter bellows

Le sorelle di mia mama,
mia mama, i mie parenti, tutti
Molti avi
ieri sera

some of you dead
some of you still living
your words flourishing wildly
in my soul

"Lesbian? *Va Nabola!* You think
you're different from us?
You think your life will be free
of pain?
*"Non farmi ridere!"**

*Don't make me laugh!

~

Giovanna Capone is a poet, fiction writer, and playwright. She was raised in an Italian American neighborhood in New York, whose strong immigrant influence still resonates in her life. She lives in California, but will always be a New York Italian. Giovanna's first book, *In My Neighborhood: Poetry & Prose From an Italian-American,* was published by Bedazzled Ink in 2014.

Her work has also appeared in various publications, including *Curaggia: Writing by Women of Italian Descent, Bless Me Father: Stories of Catholic Childhood, Unsettling America: An Anthology of Contemporary Multicultural Poetry, Avanti Popolo: Italian-American Writers Sail Beyond Columbus, Queer View Mirror 2, Lesbian & Gay Short Short Fiction,* and *Fuori: Essays by Italian/American Lesbians and Gays.* Her short fiction has appeared in the 2012 issue of *The Paterson Literary Review.*

Giovanna co-edited *Hey Paesan! Writing by Lesbians & Gay Men of Italian Descent* with Tommi Avicolli Mecca and Denise Nico Leto and *Dispatches from Lesbian America.* Giovanna lives in Oakland, CA and works as a public librarian. You can reach her at this website: http://www.giovannacapone.com.

New Hope
Pascal Scott

WHEN I WAS young and still believed that people can change, I took a job in a clinic for substance abusers called New Hope. I was the first person the New Hopefuls saw when they walked in the front door with their court-ordered referrals in their shaky hands; I did intake, which is just another way of saying I got the dirt on them before I turned them over to the counselors.

There were nineteen therapists at the clinic—thirteen middle-aged women and six middle-aged men—and they had all been addicts of one kind or another in their prime. With most it had been booze but with some it had been drugs—meth or coke, smack or ludes. Their substance of choice didn't really matter, they told me; what mattered now was that they were clean and sober; they were working the steps and making amends and reaching out to their fellow alcoholics, their sister drug addicts. I nodded and told them they were right about that, but when I went home at the end of the day I drank my wine and tried to forget all the stories I'd heard at New Hope.

I was paid eight dollars an hour for a forty-hour week, and when I finished with house payments and bills and my student loans, I had just enough money left over for staples. There was a bakery next door where I could buy a day-old loaf of French bread for fifty cents; next door to the bakery a liquor store stocked whiskey and beer and cheap wine. My habit was *Poseur Chardonnay*, an off-label brand I'd discovered on a lower shelf. At two dollars a bottle, I could rationalize a purchase three or four times a week.

New Hope was run by a tall, white-haired psychiatrist whose perfect manners and paternal air had impressed me during my two-hour job interview. But as the counselors would later remind me, things are often not what they seem. Dr. Jonathan

Hillman—he insisted we use his full title—suffered from Narcissistic Personality Disorder, a diagnosis confided to me by Manuel Luna, the clinic's only bilingual counselor.

"*Chica*," he said, his pet name for all females under thirty—of the staff that meant only me but, of course, there were his clients—"Dr. Hillman is *classic*."

He opened a thick, blue book, the most recent *Diagnostic and Statistic Manual of Mental Disorders*, flipping pages as he spoke. "Jonathan Hillman is *the* classic definition. He fits all the criteria. Listen to this:

1) Inflated self image.
2) Exploitative.
3) Insouciant temperament.

Manuel looked up from the page. "Insouciant means he doesn't care," he said.

"I know," I replied.

He cocked his head and came conspiratorially close to where I sat at my desk. He moved easily, like a dancer, like a much younger man.

"I was an English major," I explained. "Minor in Psychology."

"I'm impressed." He continued reading.

4) Cognitive expansiveness.
5) Deficient social conscience.

"That's Jonathan," he concluded. "A walking personality disorder."

I shrugged. "Who said 'We're all crazy here'?"

"I don't know," he said. "Sounds smart." He gave me his flirtatious, signature-Manuel smile—the one that worked on most of the women and some of the men. "Maybe *I* did," he said.

IN THOSE DAYS—the year was 1978—I lived a short drive from New Hope in a trailer park that abutted The Blessed Mother Cemetery in Colma, population 1,002. Back then The Blessed Mother was one of Colma's eleven places of final rest. The town's many cemeteries—nine human and two pet—had earned it a place in the *Guinness Book of Records*. The joke locally was that there were more dead people in Colma than living, which was ridiculously true. After I had moved into my double-wide, I put a bumper sticker on my truck that read, "It's good to be alive in Colma."

At twenty-eight I didn't mind living next door to a cemetery. At that point in my life I was completely unacquainted with death, and the real estate of the dead held a dark appeal for me. A cemetery seemed like a good place to go when the world closed in, and I sometimes walked the grounds at dusk. I found a preternatural calm at that hour, and if there were indeed ghosts among the headstones, I felt somehow comforted by that notion and not at all disturbed by their presence.

ONE SUMMER MORNING, a girl drifted into the clinic on a mist, or so it seemed. New Hope was located in Pacifica, a foggy beach town that lingered like an afterthought between the business centers of San Francisco to the north and San Jose to the south. The cemeteries and lone trailer park of Colma sat about ten miles to the east. To the west there was nothing but the gray-blue expanse of the Pacific Ocean.

The town had been built by old San Francisco money, and the beach cottages that once provided a weekend escape to bankers and socialites and compromised judges were now mortgaged as primary residences to blue-collar workers who struggled to make their payments. The apartment buildings had come later and with them the tatters at the end of the middle class: renters who worked for the county, the school district, or the clinic where drunks went when it was time to sober up.

That morning it had been misty since dawn, and when she walked in, the girl seemed to bring the atmosphere in with her. I checked her out; I couldn't help myself. She didn't look like one of our usual clients with their beaten-down expressions and bloodshot eyes. She looked, well, *different* wasn't quite the right adjective. Unique, maybe. This was the seventies, and Gothic was a word rarely used outside American Literature classes. But here she was in front of me: Goth before there was Goth. She was dressed entirely in black—unusual itself in a beach town— and the black of her dress matched the black of her hair, which was long and shiny and pulled back with a black ribbon. Her eyes, made wide with eyeliner, were the color of seaweed. Her lips were blood-red. Her skin was so pale it seemed almost translucent. She was stunning.

I realized with something like a small electric shock that I had not had a date in longer than I could remember. My last girlfriend had left me abruptly after persuading me to move from my hometown in Westwood—where we had both attended UCLA—to *her* hometown in S.F. Almost as soon as we'd arrived, she'd taken up with a lover from high school, and that was that. I'd lived in Victorians in the Mission with a brood of mismatched roommates until I'd saved enough for a down payment on the mobile home. It occurred to me now that I hadn't dated in months, or maybe it had been years. I'd been celibate for so long I'd lost track.

I opened a manila folder and began filling in the intake form.

"Name?" Jag Ärhon.

That sounded vaguely Nordic to me. *Funny, you don't look Nordic*. Bet it wasn't the name her mother gave her.

"Address and phone number?" She gave the address of a sketchy apartment complex up the hill, rumored by the counselors to be a shooting gallery. Not safe. But maybe she liked not safe.

"Birthdate?" She was twenty-one. A baby.

Then the question they all hated. "And what brings you to the clinic today, Ms. Ärhon?"

She pulled a piece of paper from a leather clutch, unfolded it, and pushed it across my desk. Ah, the Court Referral. I had been at New Hope only a few months and already I'd seen the Court Referral a hundred times. The letterhead told me it was from the Superior Court of California, County of San Mateo County; that Jag Ärhon was the defendant; and that she had been convicted of the misdemeanor of Driving Under the Influence with a point thirteen blood alcohol. Ouch. Under Disposition Information I read:

> Summary probation for five years. One hundred and eighty days confinement. Confinement suspended. One hundred dollar fine, alcohol related program for first offenders, license restricted for ninety days.

Bad girl. "Anything else we should know?" I asked.

"I'm a drag," she said. Only it didn't sound like "drag." She drew it out so that it sounded like "drao-ga."

I laughed and closed the folder. "Don't be too hard on yourself," I said. She didn't react, not even a smile. *No sense of humor.* Okay, maybe she *is* Nordic.

"A counselor will be with you in a few minutes. You can wait over there." I nodded toward the padded folding chairs by the front windows. The mist hadn't lifted, even though it was now late in the morning. Instead, it seemed to be hovering outside, almost as if it were waiting for something.

Jag got up then in the most peculiar manner. She didn't really *stand* up; it was more as if she *floated* up. Then she glided toward a chair to wait.

I literally shook my head. *Weird.* I looked around, but no one seemed to have noticed. I walked the folder over to Brad, an aging surfer-boy type. He glanced up from his paperwork and frowned. Sobriety didn't agree with Brad. He'd gotten his ten-year chip just a week before, but I could tell he was one of those dry drunks who would give anything to be able to hit the tequila one more time.

"She's waiting," I said. He flipped open Jag's file and skimmed it.

"Thanks," he said, not looking up.

I went back to my desk, trying to ignore the long-forgotten sensation starting between my thighs. I glanced at the girl. She had her head down, looking at an AA pamphlet she'd pulled from a display rack. *Oh yeah*, I thought, *I remember.*

MY DOUBLE-WIDE SAT in the far northeast corner of the park on an odd-shaped lot that accommodated the boundary between the residential zone of what management called my "mobile home community" and the commercial zone of The Blessed Mother Cemetery. The home's previous owner had built raised beds in the V of the twenty-by-twenty-by-thirty patch next to my unit and had planted rose bushes in the amended soil. The evening after I'd met Jag, I decided against my usual walk through The Blessed Mother and worked, instead, in the garden. I had checked out a book from the County Library—this was decades before the Internet—and had learned the types of plantings I had found there: Floribunda, Hybrid Tea, Climbing, Shrub, and Miniature. There was a kind of poetry to roses, I discovered, even in their names: Wildflower and William Shakespeare, Peter Pan and Pearl Drift, Mermaid and Magic Carpet, Claret and Tequila Sunrise.

That evening I pruned and weeded and cut a single, long-stemmed American Beauty. Inside, I ran fresh water from the kitchen faucet and filled an empty wine bottle. I slipped in the rose and took it to my room. Across from my bed on a thrift-store chest of drawers I set the makeshift vase. The rose was the last thing I saw before I turned out the light.

I usually sleep well, but that night I lay awake thinking about Jag. Uncontrollably, my thoughts obsessed about her skin. It was so—white. *White as the foam of a crashing wave. White as the silk lining of a casket.* Images flooded my brain. I pictured her white skin and imagined my tongue on her neck, gliding up under her chin, coming to rest on her mouth. That luscious, red mouth. Beneath my hips the sheets grew damp. I slid my hand between my legs and began stroking. It had been a long time. A few moments later I came in a spasm of release. My back arched and then relaxed, and I fell into a dark sleep.

I dreamed, and in the dream I was moving through a watery shadowland. The shadows were gray and green in color and seemed to exist in some bottomless, fluid space. I could hear myself breathing, but what I breathed in did not feel like air. I was breathing the liquid itself. It was as if my lungs were drawing oxygen from the water. I became aware next of my heart, which was beating as if it were flying through a tunnel, through a passageway constructed of bones.

Ahead I saw something luminescent. This unidentifiable, shining thing was a deep shade of blue except at the center, where it glowed with a white light. It, too, seemed to be liquid or nearly so, like a jellyfish. It swayed lightly where it hung suspended as if responding to some movement of water or air.

The jellyfish-like creature floated toward me and when it was within inches of my face, it metamorphosed into a seal. Yes, it was a seal now, black and slick with huge, plaintive eyes. As I watched, the eyes widened and turned seaweed-green. I blinked, and when I looked again, the seal had transformed once more and was now a familiarly beautiful girl. "Mine," she said loud enough to wake me.

I sat up like Lazarus. My heart was racing, my breath coming in shallow gasps. The sheets had sweat-soaked through to the mattress. I fumbled with the switch on my nightstand lamp. The light seemed extraordinarily bright. I lowered the lids of my eyes to let my pupils adjust. When I opened them wide, they came to rest on the vase across the room. I saw that sometime during the night, the American Beauty had died. Inexplicably, next to it there was a second rose, a rose so darkly red it was nearly black. I didn't recognize it at all and had no memory of placing it there. Confused and questioning my sanity, I pulled the library book from the nightstand and searched the pages until I found a picture that matched. I read:

> One of the deepest, darkest red roses grown, its large velvety head opens into a captivating star-shaped bloom. The Black Magic Rose.

I looked again at Black Magic and my dead American Beauty. I closed the book, turned out the light, and lay down. Maybe I was still dreaming. That must be it. In the morning everything would be back to normal.

And it was. When light broke in through my bedroom window, my room was just as it had been the evening before. The American Beauty Rose bloomed in the wine bottle. There was no Black Magic. It had been a dream.

AS PART OF their program, first offenders were required to attend AA meetings. "Ninety meetings in ninety days," the counselors told them. In the Bay Area there were so many recovering alcoholics that there were designated meetings for just about everyone's preference: men, women, youth; lesbian, gay, transgender; *En Español*; Deaf, wheelchair accessible; smokers. You could find a lesbian-only meeting any day of the week. One of these was held at New Hope. A few minutes before five every Friday evening, between twenty and thirty dykes would come through our front door, heading for the back room. The first Friday after I'd done her intake, Jag joined them. I hadn't been sure, but now it was confirmed.

Although that didn't mean much. Other than her intake stats, I didn't know anything about her. Maybe she had a girlfriend. Maybe she was a serial killer. I wasn't sure which of those prospects was more disturbing. There was a rule at the clinic against dating clients, of course, but that was written specifically for counselors. I was just the receptionist so, technically, it didn't apply to me. Even so, my conscience told me it would be wrong to hit on Jag. My body told me something else. I decided to listen to my body. I just wouldn't tell anyone, especially not the counselors. Therapists were notorious gossips, I'd learned, and if I told one, it would be all over New Hope and eventually reach Dr. Hillman.

That would mean a closed-door, one-on-one sit-down with my boss. Dr. Hillman would want to "explore" why I'd felt it necessary to violate professional standards. I'd already had one of these mandatory sessions—my indiscretion had been "laughing inappropriately." It was Manuel who got me into trouble, naturally, telling me a bad joke and then slipping away like a lover in the night. ("How many psychiatrists does it take to change a light bulb? Only one, but the light bulb really has to *want* to change.") I had left the thirty-five-minute-long meeting with Dr. Hillman feeling shamed and manipulated. Manuel was right. The clinic was run by a walking personality disorder, just as he'd said.

No, I'd keep Jag to myself and not tell anyone.

MY PLANS FOR a slow, romantic seduction did not execute exactly as I had expected. It seemed that Jag had plans of her own. One of my duties was balancing the books, something I felt singularly ill-equipped to do. The office manager was in charge of bookkeeping, but Dr. Hillman had assigned me the task of checking her work. Math has never been my strong suit, and when the numbers didn't reconcile, I would stay late until they did. Like the rest of the staff, I had a key to the front door and was able to lock up when I was the last one to leave.

That happened one Friday evening. The AA dykes had drifted out, and when I looked at the clock over Dr. Hillman's desk, I saw that its hands had somehow moved into the seven o'clock position. It was late. There was something wrong with the balance, but I couldn't find the problem. *Fuck it.* I decided to deal with it on Monday, even though I knew that would cost me another sit-down with my narcissistic boss.

I closed the blinds on the front windows. I dead-bolted the door, something I was supposed to have done more than an hour ago. Dr. Hillman was extraordinarily paranoid about getting robbed, although I thought he was somewhat justified. Substance abusers are notoriously susceptible to impulsive behavior, especially regarding the financing of their habit. We had that den of druggies just up the road and, of course, there were our clients. I put the week's revenue into the cash box, locked it, and placed it along with the ledger into the safe by Dr. Hillman's desk.

I was the only one left in the building. As I moved toward the back, turning out desk lamps as I went, I saw what I thought was a shadow. As I neared it, the shadow stepped out of a corner of darkness.

"Jag!" I said. "Jesus! You scared the crap out of me." And then I self-corrected, even though I was absolutely sure Jag's mouth was less than virginal in tongue. "Sorry. You startled me."

Amazingly, she didn't respond. *What's with this girl?*

She stared at me with those foxfire eyes. *Christ.* There was something not right about her, something dimly menacing.

"You need to leave," I said.

Still nothing. *Okay, fine. Be that way. You're a damned woman of mystery.* Drunks and druggies, I should have known better. She was gorgeous, but this fantasy of mine was crazy. At the same time, though, I was aware of a pulsing starting in my clit. *Damn.* Brain and body were at war, again.

She came at me like a storm. One second she was standing in front of me and in the next I was on my back on a counselor's desk. And the stupidest part was what I was thinking. Which was not, *why am I letting this woman fuck me like this?* Or, *what if Dr. Hillman comes back for some reason and walks in on us?*

No, it was *maybe we should move to my own desk. I don't want my juices all over somebody else's workspace.*

Because fucking was what we were doing. It wasn't lovemaking, it wasn't even sex. It was raw, hard, animalistic fucking, and I was flowing like a river that had been finally undammed. She pushed inside me until I swore I felt her hand up to her wrist. Her other hand went over my mouth, which was making sounds I'd never made before, cries I barely recognized as coming from me. She was stronger than I had expected and rougher. She was more than rough. She was almost violent with me. Her kisses were not kisses; they were bites. She bit my lip until I tasted blood. She ribbed open my shirt and sucked my nipples until they split. At the pain I gasped and opened my eyes. It's hard to describe what I saw. Her expression was catlike now, as if I were her prey. I felt an energy press itself against my chest and enter me; my body rocked and bucked, and I lifted up and went into some astral plane of light and silence. It was so peaceful there, so quiet . . .

Then I was back in my body. Jag had stepped back from me. She looked at me now, and her eyes were different. They had changed again. In them I saw satisfaction, which I had expected, but I also saw sadness, which I hadn't. I didn't understand this girl at all.

I couldn't move. I heard more than saw her walk to the front door and let herself out. It took me awhile to recover. I had to breathe in and out, in and out, and let the world come back. It was only then that I realized something. During the whole encounter, Jag hadn't said a word.

ON MONDAY, SHE missed her appointment with Brad. He tried calling her number, but it had been disconnected. Jag never returned to the clinic. I resisted the impulse for a few days, but then I gave in and walked to her apartment. A bald man with a Russian accent saw me and said it was empty and was I interested in renting? I told him no, but did he happen to know what became of the girl who lived there? He didn't. But if I saw her, she owed him money.

My life reverted to what it had been before Jag. After a while the whole incident took on the quality of a dream. As the days and then months passed into autumn, I began to wonder if it had happened at all.

But by then, the changes had started. My body soured to the smell of old milk. Sunlight hurt my eyes; air stung my lungs. A miasma of vapors seemed to follow me wherever I went. My sleep troubled with nightmares. During the day I dozed at my desk. Dr. Hillman took me to the back room to discuss the changes in my behavior. I came close to telling him to go fuck himself.

At the library I looked up my symptoms in a book on medical conditions. What I had sounded like allergies. Or asthma. Or depression. As I was setting the book in the reshelf cart, my vision focused on a volume entitled *The Ancient Art of Black Magick*. I don't know why exactly, but I picked it up and flipped it open. It fell randomly to a page. On it I read:

> DRAUGR. From Old Norse: *draugr*, plural *draugar*; literally "again-walker." The draugr is an undead creature from Norse mythology.
>
> Unlike ghosts, draugar have a corporeal body with similar physical abilities as in life. They are prone to have an appetite for food, wine, and the pleasures of the flesh. They are fluid shape-shifters, often taking the form of a seal or a cat. Draugar leave the grave to seek a victim. They can be physically and emotionally threatening to the living. They are known to cause madness in humans and animals. By infecting victims with their blood, draugar gain the ability to reproduce. A person bitten by a draugr turns into a draugr himself. Notably, a menacingly sinister cry is emitted by the victim upon the act of transmission.

I closed the book. A sick feeling had started in my stomach. I made it to the bathroom just in time. I rinsed out my mouth at the sink and looked into a cracked mirror. Draugr. *I'm a draugr.* She had warned me, and I had just hadn't heard her.

THAT WINTER I discovered what had been wrong with the books. The problems hadn't gone away; in fact, they had become more stubborn. Despite my inaptitude for accounting, I had solved the puzzle at last. Dr. Hillman was embezzling funds. That was the only explanation. Money came in from clients; Dr. Hillman used it to pay invoices he created with a little cut-and-paste, correction fluid, and the copy machine. When I put it together that way, the numbers made sense. As soon as he realized I knew, Dr. Hillman fired me. He walked me to the door without even letting me say good-bye to Manuel or Brad or anyone else.

I didn't look for another job. I slept most of the days and wandered The Blessed Mother at night. I knew what I was searching for so that when I found it, it was more of a confirmation than a surprise. On a mossy, gray tombstone I read: "Jag Ärhon. 1957-1978." The dirt around the grave had been disturbed, and there were footprints leading away toward my trailer park.

I returned the next evening. On the grave I lay an American Beauty Rose.

IT IS SPRING now. There is something so promising about spring. The loneliness of winter ends as the first buds appear. Something in the earth comes forth. Something dormant turns green. Jag Är Hon. *I Am She.*

This evening I pricked my finger on a thorn and bled. I'll wait a little longer, and then I'll start a hunt of my own. I'll know her when I catch her scent. She may look like Jag, or she may look like me. Then again, she may look just like you.

Pascal Scott is the pseudonym of a Decatur, Georgia-based writer whose erotic and romantic lesbian fiction has appeared in *Harrington Lesbian Literary Quarterly* and *In Posse Review* as well as the anthologies *Thunder of War, Lightning of Desire* and *Through the Hourglass*. Her literary fiction and poetry have been published in *Mississippi Review*, *Beloit Poetry Journal*, *The Iowa Review* and other journals.

My Wife's Ghost
By Andrea Lambert

BEFORE HER GHOST rose to obsess me, she was my wife. Katie Jacobson: twenty-three-year-old gold star lesbian from a well-off East Coast family. Educated at Occidental College and CalArts. Katie was a fellow CalArts Creative Writing MFA. Entered the program a few years after I graduated. I met Katie in 2008 through a mutual friend: Stephen van Dyck. Stephen hosted a series of parties we both attended. Katie was Stephen's friend from their dorm at Occidental college. At his best man toast at our wedding, Stephen said he always knew this union was inevitable.

Katie entered my life when she moved to North Hollywood and entered the CalArts MFA program for her first year. 2009. My abusive relationship with a meth-addled transgender prostitute was falling apart. I was about to have two books published and go on disability.

Katie rescued me from a party where my soon-to-be ex-boyfriend was going to beat me. Drove me home in her car. A few days later when my boyfriend had moved out, I invited her over to visit meet my rat babies. We went to Necromance on Melrose. Our first date was macabre romance. At my birthday party I pounced. Katie stayed the night in my arms. We were inseparable since.

Four years. For four years Katie slept by my side in that wooden four poster left by my schizophrenic grandfather. We moved in together after the first six months. Left our respective North Hollywood hovels for a back house on a compound in hipster Silver Lake. Celebrated Thanksgiving and Christmas in a honeymoon with friends for six months. It was there in Silver Lake Katie proposed, after sex one night.

When the compound fell apart we moved together to an Echo Park one bedroom with a mud room that we transformed into a dining room. We had many dinner parties and holidays there. Sent out elaborate joint photograph Christmas cards with the pets in costume. We built a life together in that hardwood-floored apartment overlooking Echo Park Lake. It was there that we won the Pink Cloud wedding contest and set about planning the wedding of our wildest dreams.

Our big beautiful gay wedding was May 14, 2011. Proposition 8 stopped its legality. Prop 8 was a stay on gay weddings from 2008 to 2013. It blocked the gay marriage legalization that had prompted Katie to propose in the first place. This required us to get a domestic partnership notarized for legality. We held the elaborate wedding ceremony we had planned anyway for the ritual and fun of things. Our wedding served no legal purpose.

We won a Pink Cloud wedding planning contest. Our wedding served a bunch of wedding vendors in getting their portfolios ready for the gay marriage landslide that was to come. Thus many vendors donated their services. The civil ceremony of our own writing was performed by my two aunts, the offici-aunts, in a Japanese Garden in Little Tokyo. We got married in downtown Los Angeles. Katie and I wore couture Louis Verdad. My best friend Omar gave me away. The invitations were letterpress. Gardenias lined black-table clothed tables with catered hors d'oeuvres. I carried a bouquet of white roses and eucalyptus. The wedding colors were white, gray, and pale green.

A year, two honeymoons and worsening alcoholism on my part later we were seeking marriage counseling. After one especially difficult fight that left me with a black eye and scratches on my wrist I awoke to find her prone, pants-less corpse next to me on the bed with vomit caked around its mouth. My wife took all of the prescription medication that I take for my mental illness and committed suicide. I was devastated. My wife killed herself to escape our marriage.

We cremated her. Had an elaborate funeral at Hollywood Forever. I remember the flowers moldering in that Echo Park apartment for months as I cried and drank.

I moved to Hollywood. Got sober through inpatient detox and outpatient rehab. I couldn't get sober for my wife anymore but I could do it for myself. I lost my wife partially because of my drinking. For the very least I could stop now. I did stop drinking.

I took up witchcraft. Got a medical marijuana card on my therapist's suggestion. I went to therapy a lot. Was still on disability.

The schizoaffective disorder that manifested through delusions, hearing voices, and seeing ectoplasmic shimmery shapes began to manifest as visitations from Katie's ghost. At first Katie's ghost was insistent, angry. She didn't want to be dead. She didn't want me to be dating a new man as I was eight months later. As I lay naked in my new boyfriend's bed Katie's ghost swirled around me. Her face appeared on the wall of his bedroom. Katie told me how sad she was to be apart from me.

At home I took down the wedding picture from the living room wall to appease my boyfriend. Katie's face formed in the empty wall space. Melding in and out of a skull. Telling me how much she loved and missed me. I lay on my bed, hallucinating on the wall. After Katie's visitation, I put the photograph back up.

My schizophrenia began to manifest solely as manifestations of my wife's ghost. I came to believe that my schizoaffective disorder gave me an edge in communicating with the other world. I honed my tarot skills. I did spells. I studied witchcraft and yoga. I sat in yoga positions in my witch hat with my hands raised in occult gestures like antennae. Listening to the voice of Katie's ghost. She told me many things.

I never see Katie as a white humanoid apparition as ghosts somehow manifest. I see her when I see her at all as a ball of energy or ectoplasm, moving across the ceiling. I have heard her voice many times. I always knew when the voice was Katie because she would call me "wuzh." Our tender secret nickname for each other.

As a schizoaffective I often hear voices. First I try to figure out who I am speaking with. Sometimes I perceive the presence as telepathy from alien gods who I imagine are above me in a flying saucer in space. Aliens talking through my mind in a conference call to check in with me. Dionysus and Persephone tell me all is well and they are pleased with my progress. Happy I am such an open vessel for them to communicate with.

Sometimes the voices in my head just identify themselves as "Oh, we're the voices in your head. You might want to put in your headphones because we're about to get talkative." Then I just put my headphones in, listen to Lana Del Rey, and tune them out. The voices I hear are encouraging, kind, helpful. They don't scare me. They comfort me. I am lucky.

Auditory psychosis strikes most often with sleep deprivation. At least once a week I stay up all night. Don't take my sleepy time schizophrenia medication. The Saphris usually puts me to sleep. Some nights when I have free time I prefer not to take the Saphris. Instead stay up all night. It is on those mornings after I have completed dawn meditation and yoga that I am most often visited by Katie's ghost. I seek these visitations. I stay up all night often. I want to talk to Katie. I want to break through to the other side. Hear her whisper in my ear.

Katie's ghost began to visit me in the first year after her death before I scattered her ashes. At the year anniversary of Katie's death, upon her ghost's urging, I scattered Katie's ashes at Echo Park Lake with an AA buddy. I reserved a small ziplock for her parents. Gave it to them at a dinner when they visited. Opening the cardboard box of ashes that had sat for a year in my drawer in a Hollywood Forever shopping bag was one of the hardest things I've ever had to do. Scattering the ashes of my dead wife into the blue and glittering water of the newly renovated lake we had so loved together and lived above for most of the relationship, I watched the ashes drift down into the green-blue water from the paddleboat. In the boat with me was: a wedding invitation, her funeral card, one of her zines.

Katie's ghost was angry and aggressive with me for a while for dating someone new and neglecting to scatter her ashes for so long. She swirled around me on a hiking trail in Griffith Park with my boyfriend. The anger continued for two weeks. Then one night I heard Katie from my boyfriend's bedroom bidding me farewell in a rising chorus of angel voices. She was rising up towards the next level in the afterlife. Bidding me farewell and love as she moved on. I thought I wouldn't hear from her after that. I was wrong.

When Katie's ghost came to me after that she was milder. She had accepted that I was dating someone new and felt that I adequately honored her. I started a short-lived small press with the intention of publishing her thesis manuscript via print-on-demand. I released Katie's zine *Vergangenheitsbewaltigung* as our second in a chapbook series that was to include three chapbooks before I dissolved the press a year later, realizing my financial resources for such a project were simply not adequate. Small presses just eat up your money. As a disabled women I must husband my resources. Katie's ghost seemed to understand this. She did not rage at me when I gave up the project.

Katie's ghost visited me from the great beyond many times, especially after late nights. Told me of the afterlife. Her further adventures as a ghost. What would likely happen upon my death.

I now include an excerpt from my unpublished novel, *Diary of a Hollywood Hedgewitch*, in which I wrote about a real-life encounter with her ghost.

II.

I HEAR VERY clearly in my head, "So now you get to be noble and I get to be dead." Katie's ghost is back. Sleep deprivation often brings this on. I don't take my schizophrenia medication and I hear voices. Of course reading that story exactly about our relationship that eerily predicted the suicide called her ghost up again, clearly.

I finish reading Katie's manuscript. Make small copyedits. Look over and approve Harold's edits. The heat is on. Bewitched plays from the TV. I am acutely sad for my dead wife who was so brilliant as to have predicted everything in this her novel from beyond the tomb. I saw myself and her again and again in reading it.

I forgive Katie for everything. She was troubled, as was I, and we were locked in a death dance where only one of us could survive. I didn't kill her. She took her own life as assuredly as she predicted again and again with the suicides of the characters in her book. When I got her laptop back, there was a background of a woman shooting herself in the head. I finally changed it after I couldn't look at it anymore.

A voice in my head chants, "Katie committed suicide because she could not be living with you in a relationship for a single second longer . . . she thought but now realizes maybe that was a bad idea."

Katie chimes in, "Because now I'm stuck in purgatory and it's shitty here, the food and table manners are so, like, institutional. It's like afterlife rehab. Basically imagine Las Encinas with more gray dust and doric columns."

"That doesn't sound that bad," I say inside my brain to her.

As I type at my desk, Katie's voice in my head says, "Okay you are so on your game writing this all down as I say? We are automatic writing? Oh it's on! Okay, so anyway, the afterlife? It's um . . . challenging. Like, we're all here in this place, and we have similar stories. It's like we just talk about our lives all the time and work things out about them. It's like an endless therapy session. Sometimes they bring in finger sandwiches or give you a mani-pedi. So, it doesn't always suck. Basically I'm just going a little stir crazy only having a few people to haunt.

"I mean, how do I put this? It's like, if you want to reunite with me in the afterlife you can, but you might have to stay in purgatory if you do. Whoosh, I want you to go to heaven with Bobby and be happy. His Catholic agnostic good guy thing and your Wicca good witch thing you will be VIP in heaven. It's not Christian faith! It isn't like the Christian faith says in the afterlife!

"It's practically like an alien subculture, the aliens that fuck with humans. They've been coming to Earth for so long. *Ancient Aliens* is right. The aliens run the afterlife, too. The chick who does my nails on Thursdays is an alien and she always has the most fascinating stories about . . . What was I talking about? Okay aliens, there's a lot of aliens in the afterlife. They seem to run everything. Just get used to it. Humans are an inferior species but still useful to study. 'Your blind faith in the gods of your ancestors is beautiful to see, all of you,' the alien above me just said. The aliens that still come here come in peace. It's a hobby for them to watch people on Earth.

"It's definitely a hobby for souls in purgatory to watch people on Earth. We are just waiting for you and Bobby to get married. Then I might be able to go to heaven to meet you guys there if I'm extra good. I mean, purgatory is a little bit like prison. It depends how long you stay on how well you play the game. I'm actually really good at this from my time at Kent Place. If I play my cards right I could be in heaven to meet you guys instead of being here in purgatory fucking about. It's like endlessly fucking about on Wikipedia on a late long night here, seriously. Before you say that doesn't sound that bad, like that could be heaven where you are and you don't realize it, I mean, maybe I'm in heaven? It seems purgatory-ish still. Maybe it will get better and I'll just kind of ease my way into a better situation here with the angels. The angels are a type of alien. The humanoid winged kind. They're mostly concerned with managing the afterlife.

"You have a book on this, that book that we bought at Illiad Books, the old spell book, but it's all . . . Oh I forgot. That one's all in Olde English and from an 1890 perspective. No, don't read that one."

"Thank you so much for telling me all this stuff," I beam off through my brain at one pm in the afternoon.

"Liveblogging on point today, bee-tee-dubs," Katie says. "You always were good at writing down what the voices in your head told you."

A car passes loudly outside. I hear my cat tapping a toy around. Thumps and bangs. Voices, cars, the typing keys, all of the ordinary human noises I had been avoiding to listen to Katie's voice. Suddenly I'm hearing the old black lady on the corner talking. Pings of e-mail coming in.

"That's nice, okay, I don't care, I don't care," I say as I go through my e-mail. "That wasn't directed at you, Katie. You can keep talking to me for as long as you want to."

"You have a lot of shit to do, wuzh. Stop listening to me and get to work," she says. I consider. Read back through what she told me. Tear up.

"Katie!" I sob.

"The porn virus, the porn virus, that porn virus," Katie says in my head. "Okay, now that I've got your attention. I want you to tell Stephen that it's going to be okay. Wait, I'll tell him that. He's getting better at hearing me now. It's a special way of hearing. You're really good at it. Shining, yes, that's what it's called sometimes. Because we're each shining in each others' minds and hearts for a moment."

I feel Katie close to me. Her presence. I look over my shoulder. Only the broken lamp from Ikea with a Mexican wrestler mask on it. The orange blur of the couch we bought together at Goodwill that Bobby wanted to replace for me.

"Nooo, don't replace the couch." Katie says. "I like haunting this couch. You sit on this couch a lot. I can hold you."

"Okay, sweetie, you can haunt the couch. Haunt it up."

"Now that you smoke pot 24/7, aren't you the sweetest person ever."

"Pretty much, yes. That might have something to do with how loud and clear I hear you. I don't know yet. It doesn't make me inclined to not smoke weed."

"Keep smoking weed. Keep smoking weed!" The rising whir of weed. Voices on the street. "I want to help you with some witchcraft."

"Okay," I think. I go to my altar. Cross my legs. Light incense and a candle. Lift my hands in the Horned God and Goddess gestures. Katie directs me to go to page 137 of *Green Witchcraft* where there is a Money spell. I turn one more page to the Health spell. I draw a circle, invoke the elements, and do a spell for the health, wholeness, and healing of Lish Pulverizer and Jessie Davis. In the final visualization I see the three of us sitting together in an outdoor café in Los Angeles. Jessie slim. Lish healthy. Three friends talking in a café that gradually spins up and out of sight. I close the circle. Snuff the candles. Sit back on the couch.

"We will have to take Lish," says the voice. "The Grim Reaper keeps going out for her and then it's only love that holds him back. Your love and that of her friends and family. Do you release her? The afterlife will be good to her and her suffering now is great. Are you ready take on the responsibility of your love being the only thing keeping her alive?"

"I release Lish to her destiny," I say. I cry.

Katie's voice comes back. "This is happened, this is happening Andrea. You need to know that Bobby is deeply in love with you but conflicted about not being able to have children with you and whether you're ever going be over me and put all the witchcraft away. He loves you, and he will marry you regardless of any of his misgivings. Remember when I told you I had psychic powers because I had a mental disorder and you told me I was crazy and should just take my medication? Well. you should probably take your schizophrenia medication eventually unless you really want to hear me all the time. But I mean, I'll hang out as long as you want to."

I hear laughing. The walls seem to be vibrating. A high streak of hilarity from a driver going by.

"You should go to sleep, yeah! You should go to sleep, yeah! You should go to sleep, yeah!" Katie repeats it over and over until I say yes. I will. It is one pm. I take my medication and sleep.

III.

WHAT THIS VISITATION as well as the other visitations have taught me is that there is an afterlife. My wife is in a good place. She loves me. Like Lana Del Rey sings, she will be "waiting on the other side." I know I will be reunited in death with my wife. I plan to live a long full life beside my boyfriend and then when I am old and gray lie down and meet up with Katie again in the great Echo Park Lake in the sky.

I am so relieved that my schizoaffective disorder is choosing to manifest as comforting visits from my wife's ghost instead of something dangerous or scary. This reassures me that the genetic burden of mental illness can be a blessing and not a curse. I have heard from others of Katie's friends that they have more trouble than I do communicating with her ghost. Katie's ghost is always trying to communicate. My wife's ghost is an active ghost. Haunting it up.

I hear souls after suicide are trapped in purgatory. I imagine it will be a long time yet that I continue to hear her. Perhaps until I join her. I am pleased by that. Resigned to be a haunted widow. Continually with one foot in the grave. Hearing voices from the afterlife. My haunting muse inspires me. I listen for her always.

~

Andrea Lambert is the author of *Jet Set Desolate, Lorazepam & the Valley of Skin* and the chapbook *G(u)ilt*. Her work has appeared in *HTMLGIANT, 3:AM Magazine, Fanzine, Entropy, Queer Mental Health*, and *Enclave*. Her poetry has been anthologized in *Writing the Walls Down:a convergence of LGBTQ Voices, Off the Rocks #16, The L.A. Telephone Book, You've Probably Read This Before*, and *Chronometry*. She is a visual artist and CalArts MFA. Find her online at andreaklambert.com.

Spirit Horse Ranch
Sacchi Green

SOMEONE WAS BEHIND her.

Emmaline, deep in the root cellar, hadn't heard Sigri's truck pull in or Chinook bark a welcome, but the sense of a presence was unmistakable. It had to be Sigri, or the dog would've sounded a warning. Sigri could sneak up on grazing elk, when the wind was right; even if Emmaline hadn't been hammering at shelves for her preserves, she might have missed any sounds. She'd been humming, too, immersed in the joy of working among provisions of her own raising. Not that she wasn't always, on some level, listening for Sigri every bit as intently as the dog did.

Sigri would sometimes press up against Emmaline from the rear with no warning, nuzzle her neck, and reach around for further fondling. If she was in the mood, why not go along with it? Emmaline lowered the hammer and moved back a step, as though surveying her handiwork. Her backside tingled in anticipation.

A touch on her hair made her jump. "You're back early," she said. "Didn't figure you'd get here from Bozeman so . . . Ouch!" Fingers tightened on her long, thick braid, and icy-cold knuckles dug into the nape of her neck. Somebody pulled, hard.

"Hey!" Emmaline tried to turn. The hidden tormentor jerked her head back viciously and yanked again. Tears burned her eyes and panic pounded in her veins.

It wasn't Sigri.

Sigri wouldn't do that. She knew enough about Emmaline's past, and the things that triggered memories. And no one else who knew would dare, or care enough, to search her out after twenty years—if he was even still alive.

Terror snapped into sudden rage. Emmaline wasn't fifteen and vulnerable any more. She kicked back sharply at ankle-height, let out a yell worthy of an old-time Blackfeet war party, and swung the hammer at what should be a thigh—or, better yet, more vulnerable parts.

Her foot didn't connect with anything. Neither did the hammer. But her yell brought Chinook scrambling down the stairs from the kitchen in a frenzy of barks and growls. Could the cellar, crowded with sacks of winter-keeping vegetables and shelves of canning jars, hold Emmaline, the intruder, and an enraged German Shepherd all at the same time?

Emmaline wrenched sideways to free herself. Resistance ceased so abruptly that she spun right around, her russet braid flipping over one shoulder. A gust of cold air rushed past; she staggered, nearly fell, and grabbed at Chinook's shoulder for balance.

Nobody was there.

A bulb dangling from a cord hooked to the ceiling lit the space well enough. None of the sacks and crates looked disturbed. Nobody could have got out past the dog, even though her growls had subsided.

"C'mon, Chinook, upstairs." Emmaline couldn't keep her voice steady. The chill where her neck had been touched crawled all the way down her back. *What if he wasn't alive—but had come for her anyway?* No! She had to get out of there, get her thoughts under control.

She moved toward the steps, overwhelmed by a desperate need for Sigri—and just as glad Sigri wasn't there to witness her weakness.

"Chinook, come!" The dog's tail wagged to show she'd heard, but she kept sniffing among the crates. Just doing her job, searching for whatever had made her mistress yell like a damn fool. But when she clambered onto a heap of potato sacks and started nosing at the packed earth wall, it was too much.

"Drat you, Chinook, come on!" The dog kept poking at the wall. Small chunks of dirt had dribbled down, a few feet to the left of the new shelves. The hammering must have jarred them loose. A few bits of old sticks or roots showed in the roughened earth, but there wasn't a hole, so far as she could tell without going closer, which she wasn't about to do. Nothing big enough to let a mouse through, much less a rat. A rat?

She bolted upward, not looking to see if the dog followed. Her scalp still stung from the tugs. No rat could have been that strong!

Better that, though, than anything else occurring to her. She could deal with vermin. Still . . . a great filthy rat clinging to her head? She scrabbled at her braided hair until it hung loose around her shoulders and shook it so hard her brains seemed to slosh like flapjack batter. Her heart pounded, anger mixing with fear. She tried hard to let the anger win out.

A bark and a high-pitched whine came up from the root cellar. Emmaline went to the top of the steps. "Get your furry butt up here," she yelled, beginning to lower the trapdoor. Chinook, not wanting to be shut below, left off whatever she was doing and bounded up into the kitchen.

"If you haven't caught 'em yet, you won't, not without tearing up my spuds and onions!" The scolding was mostly to keep her own voice steady. "Wait for Sigri to get home!"

At the sound of that name, the dog padded hopefully to the screen door and looked out at the empty, dusty road connecting the ranch to the rest of the world. For all her devotion to Emmaline, Chinook looked to Sigri as her one true goddess.

No argument there, Emmaline thought. To see Sigri riding against the backdrop of the mountains, lithe, strong, the herd of horses running with her for the pure joy of it, any passing stranger might think Montana was as close to heaven as Earth could get. At night, in ways no passerby could imagine, Emmaline knew for sure she'd found her own personal paradise.

But what was she going to tell Sigri? That she'd freaked out in the root cellar, thought about ghosts, when it might be just rats? Even in the familiar normalcy of the kitchen, she couldn't really believe that. Whatever she decided, it would go better after supper, and there wouldn't be any supper if she didn't get on with it.

Chicken and dumplings had been her plan, with leftovers from the hen she'd roasted Sunday. But she'd forgotten to bring carrots and onions up from the cellar. Forgotten? Well, not exactly, but nothing was going to get her down into that hole again just yet.

That hole? Now anger did win out. She'd been so proud of the root cellar, clearing out generations of trash, building shelves and bins, reinforcing the support posts and steps with Sigri's help. It was older than the ranch house itself, part of a pioneer dugout home carved into the hillside. Most of it had caved in well over a hundred years ago, but when Sigri's great-great-grandfather had built his house of red cedar logs the kitchen had overlapped what was left of the hole just enough for the trapdoor and stairs to connect with it. Back then it had been used as a root cellar, but not in recent years.

Emmaline had found things in the rubble that could have been there since before the cave-in. Once she'd dug out a flat tin box, barely protruding from the wall, and found inside two long, faded coils of hair, one blonde, one reddish. Maybe two girls sick with the fever had needed to have their hair cut when it got too tangled, as was common in the old days. In an odd way it had given her a sense of connection to those long-ago settlers. She might not belong here in any conventional way—she knew the townsfolk preferred to think of her as Sigri's housekeeper and business manager, nothing closer—but she did belong to the tradition of growing and harvesting and tending loved ones.

Which included making supper. Question was, could Emmaline let herself be scared out of her own root cellar by . . . well, once she knew for sure what it was, maybe she wouldn't be so scared.

For now, there was plenty left of the big kettle of chili Sigri cooked once a week. Emmaline could whip up a batch of cornbread and pull some greens from the autumn garden. Sigri wouldn't object, having pretty much lived on nothing else in the years she'd ranched here alone.

A tensing of the dog's back, a perking of ears, brought Emmaline to the screen door. Dust puffed in the distance, where the road was no more than a crease in grasslands tinted gold by the afternoon light. Beyond, blue mountains streaked with early snow rose in jagged ranges; the Absarokee and Beartooth to the south, the Crazies to the west. To Emmaline they were guardians, shielding her against where she'd come from, who she'd had to be; but even their grandeur dimmed behind the glint of sunlight on the approaching truck.

Chinook's whines rose to a frantic pitch. It didn't take the dog's quivering rump, ready to break out into a fit of wagging, to tell Emmaline that the truck was Sigri's. She knew, as surely as the dog, and she understood the impulse to race to meet the loved one, but Chinook, for all her size, was barely out of puppyhood and still needed her training reinforced. Her job, her sacred charge, was to stay close to Emmaline every minute.

Sigri had swapped the stud service of her Appaloosa stallion for the pick of a neighbor's litter of pups. "Folks around here are pretty much decent, mind-their-own-business types, whatever their beliefs," she'd said, "but punks can sprout up anywhere, even Montana. A good dog can make 'em think twice about trying to get at . . . well, at a woman out here alone."

No need to spell it out. It wasn't just being a woman alone. What had happened down in Laramie to that boy Matthew Shepard was on both their minds. Sigri, when she'd lived alone, hadn't worried; nearly everybody within fifty miles was related to her, or owned horses she'd trained. She was one of their own. Emmaline, for all her farm-girl background, wasn't.

The red truck was close enough now for her to make out the familiar lines. Where the road dipped down to ford the tree-lined creek, green-gold leaves hid it for a moment; this was when Emmaline would generally head out to open the gate in the stock fence. Right now she wasn't sure her legs would take her that far without some wobbling Sigri was sure to notice.

"Stay!" She pressed her hand down hard on Chinook's wriggling shoulders. Sigri reached the gate, got out to open it herself, looked searchingly up at the house, and got back in. Emmaline waited until the truck stopped between the barn and the house and then, finally, let Chinook out.

Sigri stood, stretched her rangy body after the bumpy ride, pushed back her Stetson until straw-pale cropped hair showed above her tanned forehead, and looked again toward the house. Glimpsing Emmaline inside the doorway, she flashed a boyish grin that would never grow old, no matter how many lines time and weather etched on her face.

The dog pranced around her legs in frantic welcome. Weanling fillies along the paddock fence whickered in greeting. Emmaline, aching to be there too, watched as each animal got its moment of affection. When Sigri finally hauled sacks of groceries out of the truck and strode toward the house, Emmaline barely had time to tie on her apron, pour flour and corn meal into a bowl, and get enough on herself to look like she'd been in the middle of mixing.

The screen door swung open and shut. As soon as the bags and a banded bundle of mail were safely on the kitchen table, and the Stetson tossed onto its hook, Emmaline proceeded to wipe her hands on the blue-checked dishtowel and rush to grab a big hug.

Sigri'd noticed something, though. "You okay, babe?" She stroked the loose tangle of hair Emmaline had forgotten to tidy. Fear came surging back.

With her arms around Sigri's lean body and her head nestled against a firm shoulder, Emmaline managed to say, "Sure I'm okay. How'd it go in Bozeman?"

"Not too bad." Sigri tried to get a look at Emmaline's face. "I dropped off your baked goods at the café. Claire wrote a check for last week and this week too, so we're all square there. And Rogers at the bank seemed pretty sure we can get an extension on the loan. He knows I'm owed enough by the horse trek outfitters to cover it."

Emmaline burrowed a little closer, then tilted her head back for a kiss. Chinook, firmly trained not to interrupt such proceedings, lay down with her head between her paws, and then, impatient, went to nose around the edges of the trapdoor.

Emmaline became vaguely aware of the rattle of some small object being pushed around the floor behind her. Sigri, looking past her shoulder, broke the clinch. "What's that dratted dog got? Chicken bone?"

"Not from my kitchen . . ." Emmaline stopped. Chinook was offering her prize to Sigri. Held tenderly, in jaws trained to pick up eggs without breaking them, was a four-inch sticklike object. Not, they both knew, a stick. Bone, but not chicken bone. Chickens don't have fingers.

Sigri knelt. "Good girl," she said, ruffling the dog's ears. She took the bone and inspected it. "Not fresh, at least. Old. Real old, I'd say, but not prehistoric. Where'd you get that?" She looked up. "Where's she been?"

Emmaline managed to yank a chair out from the table and slump into it. "Just here, in the house, or right beside me outdoors. And . . . down in the root cellar. I was putting up some more shelves."

Sigri's long body straightened. She hauled out a chair, straddled it backwards, and surveyed Emmaline keenly. "Down in the dugout? Guess you must have been hammering up some storm to get yourself so bedraggled."

"Well, I was," Emmaline said, steadying herself with pure stubbornness. "I built a good strong set of shelves. And maybe shook a little dirt lose from the wall, but I swear there wasn't any crack big enough for . . . for a rat."

"What's a rat got to do with it?"

"Nothing!" Emmaline fastened her hair back tight with the rubber band from the bundle of mail. A couple of magazines unfurled to show covers she wouldn't have wanted the local postmistress to see, which, along with the occasional specialty mail order delivery, was why they kept a post office box in the university town of Bozeman.

"Then why'd you mention it? Come on, Em, tell me what's been going on."

Emmaline drew a deep breath, let it out, and tried again. "I don't know. Maybe one of those flashback things like they write about. But I was feeling so happy right then, safe, my preserves and vegetables all set for winter . . . and when I felt somebody behind me I figured it was you." She reached out a hand. In an instant Sigri's fingers were warm and firm on hers.

"But it wasn't you," Emmaline went on. "Somebody . . . something . . . yanked hard on my hair, pulled my head right back, just like that old bastard used to do. I yelled and swung the hammer and jerked around, and . . . nobody was there. Just Chinook, scrambling down the stairs growling fit to scare a bear from its den."

Sigri looked a shade paler under her tan, but her voice held steady. "Good for her!" She stood to pull Emmaline into another hug. "So what's this about the rats?"

"Nothing, really. She just went poking and whining at the rough spot in the wall, and wouldn't come upstairs until I started to close the trapdoor. So I thought of rats, and wondered if one could have jumped on me."

"Do you still reckon that was it?" Sigri was so close her breath warmed Emmaline's cheek. Emmaline wished she could never be any farther away, although warming other bits of her anatomy would be just fine.

"I . . . well, I don't believe in ghosts any more than you do, so . . ." She stopped, feeling a slight tensing of Sigri's body. "But . . . you don't, do you?"

"Don't I? Can't say as I recall ever discussing that particular subject." Sigri didn't seem about to say any more.

Emmaline made a lame attempt at humor. "Well, generally you're so level-headed snow could build up a foot deep and not slide off if I didn't tip you over from time to time."

It worked. Sigri chuckled. "If it's tipping you've got on your mind, girl . . ." She lifted Emmaline right off her feet and up until that warm mouth was pressed right between her breasts. The long, slow slide back down was so sweet and tantalizing it could almost make them both forget what else was on their minds. Almost.

The fingerbone lay on the table, seeming to point right at them. Emmaline itched to knock it off, kick it out the door, and scrub both table and floor.

Sigri sighed and set her down. "Guess I'd better check things out. My grandmother wouldn't go in that cellar on a bet, always had a strange feeling about it, but I never paid any heed." She hoisted up the trapdoor fast, as if in a hurry to get it over with before she changed her mind. "Looks like you left the light on down there."

"I guess I did." The hole was swallowing Sigri feet first as she went down the stairs. Emmaline hurried to the edge to keep sight of her.

"Hang onto the dog," Sigri called from below. "Danged mutt seems to have clawed out a fair bit more before you got her upstairs."

Emmaline, already gripping Chinook's collar, nearly asked, "A fair bit of what?" But she already had far too good a notion. "Bones?" she managed to croak.

"Yep, looks like two hands, most of an arm, and signs of more where those came from. Don't worry, though." Sigri glanced up over her shoulder and flashed a wan imitation of a grin. "I haven't been stashing the remains of my exes in the wall. These've been here for a mighty long time."

"They'll keep, then, till the sheriff or somebody can take them away," Emmaline said sharply. Fear was rising again, but not so much for herself. "Sigri, please, come on back up here." She moved down a step, still holding the dog back. Chilly air gripped her ankles.

Sigri, bending over the jumble of dirt and bone fragments and rotted scraps of cloth, didn't answer. Emmaline took another step downward.

Sigri's head jerked sharply back. She let out a strangled yell, kicked wildly at thin air, and clawed at her own throat. Emmaline and Chinook took the stairs in three mad leaps. By the time they got to her Sigri was flat on her back, writhing, cursing, flailing with arms and knees at an unseen attacker.

The dog snarled and whirled, not knowing what to lunge at. Emmaline, without any thought at all, flung herself right over Sigri and hung on as though she could ward off the attack with her own flesh. Maybe it worked. Something so cold it burned, streaked along her back, and was gone.

Sigri's breath came in such tearing gasps that Emmaline raised up to a crouch so as not to smother her.

"It's okay," Emmaline soothed, hoping fervently that she was right. "We're okay, it's gone." The dog was barking right at the wall now, as though some malevolent force had retreated back into the earth.

Sigri struggled to sit up. Emmaline backed off and stood up. Sigri took her hand, got to her feet, and shook herself like a dog who'd rolled in dirt. Or carrion.

"Em . . ." She tried again. "Whatever . . . whatever's going on, looks like we're in it together."

"You're damned right. But we can just as well be in it together upstairs." She tugged Sigri toward the steps, and Chinook, foreseeing the closing of the trapdoor, followed them quickly.

"Get out of those clothes," Emmaline ordered, "and into the shower. Then we'll call the sheriff's office, and after that you'll tell me every last thing you've ever heard about the dugout." It might not make sense, but somehow knowing that she wasn't alone in this steered her away from panic and into problem-solving mode.

"How about you get your clothes off, too," Sigri said, clearly beginning to recover, "and we'll talk about it in the shower together."

Emmaline hadn't realized until that moment that she too had been rolling in that unspeakable filth on the cellar floor, or at least crouching in it. "Great idea," she said.

But the supply of hot water was limited, and the need to cling together in the warm, sheltering flow was intense, so not that much talking got done. "Em, are there marks on my throat?" Sigri asked after a while.

Emmaline checked. "No bruises that I can see. A few scratches, likely from your own fingernails. What . . . what was it like?"

"Just . . . well, scrabbling at my hair, at first, and then choking, and then . . . knocking me down, poking, trying to touch places . . ." Sigri faltered.

"Places nobody but me gets to touch," Emmaline said grimly. "Could be he thought from your short hair you were a man, and then got the notion maybe you weren't and was set on finding out." She touched her lips to several of the areas in question, very gently at first until Sigri wasn't so tense, at least not in the same way, and then applied them to the hollow of her throat with such fervor that there soon *would* be some interesting marks. Sigri held her even tighter, but the water was cooling, and neither of them was in a state to tolerate chills.

When they'd dried off, dressed, and steeled themselves to get on with it, Emmaline handed the phone to Sigri.

They hadn't discussed what to say. Sigri kept to the bare facts as coolly as anybody could who'd found a body buried in their cellar. "Must have been somebody caught in that cave-in back in eighteen-whatever. Early seventies, I think. Before my people got here. Anyway, I figure that's your department, or the coroner's, or maybe some archaeologist's. Appreciate it if you'd come out and take a look." There was a pause. "Well, we sure do want it out of there, but I guess it's not likely to go anywhere before morning. See you then. And Frank . . . say howdy to Shirley for me."

"Tomorrow," Emmaline said flatly. "Well, all right then." The sheriff and his wife were cousins of Sigri's to one degree or another, just like most everybody in the county. Two or three had come up to Emmaline on the street in town to say hello, and go on a bit about Sigri having somebody to feed her up and get her accounts in order. There'd been no mention of visits, but things could have been worse.

"Should I . . ." Sigri made as if to dial the phone again.

"No, you did right. The rest is purely our own business. But . . . how about we sleep in the barn tonight."

Chinook was nosing uneasily around the edges of the trapdoor. Sigri nodded. "Good idea. Talking of the barn, I've got chores to do before dark."

Emmaline gave up any thought of cooking, and went to help herd the weanlings inside and feed all the critters that needed feeding. Sigri got fed cold chicken and leftover biscuits.

The barn was warm with the breath and smell of horses, the sweet scent of hay. Warm and safe, as they snuggled together under wool blankets. "Tell me about the old dugout now, and the cave-in," Emmaline said.

Sigri was still shaken, and not hiding it. The times when she opened up, let some vulnerability show, told Emmaline most surely what she meant to the tough rancher.

"I never listened a lot to old stories when I was a kid," Sigri said. "Always trailing after the men and the horses, learning from them, not putting much stock in women's talk. There was one thing, though . . ." She hesitated. "Well, you asked about believing in ghosts. They said it was a horse caved in that dugout, stomped on top of it, broke his legs and likely had to be shot. A big one, crossbred draft horse—my grandad's grandad hauled away the bones from on top of the rubble when he bought the land."

"Nobody dug to see if anybody'd been caught inside?"

"Not that I know of. That was some years after it happened. But folks seemed sure the people living there, two young brothers wintering over on the way to try their luck in Canada, got out okay and traveled on."

"So . . . where does the ghost part come in?"

Sigri drew in a deep, slow breath.

"Have you ever wondered why I call this place Spirit Horse Ranch?" Emmaline hadn't wondered. It had just seemed . . . right. But Sigri didn't wait for an answer. "I've seen spirit horses, times when nobody else could. And I've seen that horse. On clear nights, under moonlight, down across the creek near the hollow where the bones got dumped. You could still see humps where the grass grew over them. After the first time, I used to ride back now and then, and mostly he'd be there. He'd lift his head and look at me, and my horse would whicker a little, and then he'd just . . . fade away. Never any footprints in the daylight, when I went back to look, even if the ground was muddy. Haven't seen him in years, though, not since the creek flooded through that hollow and washed away everything, bones and all."

"So maybe getting rid of the bones gets rid of the ghost." Emmaline was trying to puzzle things out.

"That'll be just fine with me!" Sigri stretched, and yawned.

Emmaline couldn't rest quite yet. "Sigri, remember that old tin box I showed you, with the hanks of hair in it?"

"Sure, one of 'em towheaded and the other a redhead like you." She nuzzled the loose russet hair on Emmaline's shoulder.

Thoughts swirled in Emmaline's mind, notions twisting themselves around a time or two and settling into a possible pattern. The ghost had grabbed her hair, and tried to grab Sigri's. Could be he was searching for somebody, somebody female.

But Sigri was nuzzling now with clear intent, and nothing could be better than to stop thinking for a while and turn to pure feeling.

If the ghost was watching—and she didn't believe he was, with his bones far away in the root cellar—let him eat his rotted heart out.

The sheriff arrived just past morning chore time. With him were the coroner, two deputies in a pickup truck, and Shirley.

Emmaline had reclaimed her kitchen before sunrise. The parts about no footprints, no bruises on Sigri's throat, and her own hair not coming loose until she'd torn at it herself, all led to the near-conviction that ghosts couldn't do you real physical harm, unless your fear did it for them. Pain, yes, that came from the mind; they could make you feel like you were being attacked, but maybe nothing more. Still, the more his bones had been dug out, the worse the assaults had felt. Digging out the whole thing might be more than anybody should have to deal with.

So she'd lifted the trap door, and carried the open tin box down just a step or two. Nothing stirred except a cold breeze. "Look," she called down into the dark. "They got away, they're long gone." She raised each coil of hair to display. "We're not the ones you're looking for!"

Safe back in the kitchen with the trapdoor shut, she peered down into the box. There'd been a tiny clink when she'd replaced the hair. She lifted the coils again and saw two small, broken, tarnished rings. The last bits of the puzzle fell into place for her, whether anybody else would believe it or not.

Then she'd fixed up enough coffee and apple cake to feed whoever came. Hadn't counted on the sheriff's wife, but her kitchen was nothing to be ashamed of, if you didn't count a body buried under one corner of it.

Shirley was vigorous, fiftyish, a rancher in her own right on land passed down through her family. Emmaline braced herself for whatever might come, but she took the woman's offered hand and shook it firmly.

"Can I call you Emmaline? Well," as Emmaline nodded, "I'm ashamed you've been here near a year and I haven't managed to stop by to say howdy. I hope you don't mind my coming today, but with all this happening it's bound to be hard for you, and I hoped maybe I could help."

Emmaline, still wary, said she was glad of the company, and after more introductions and much hearty appreciation of coffee and cake, the trapdoor was raised.

"Emmaline," Shirley said kindly, "maybe we could head down by the barn while they tramp around in here. You could show me the new crop of young'uns. Nobody breeds horses as fine as Sigri's."

By the time they reached the paddock Emmaline had made some hard decisions. "Shirley," she said, "I'm real glad to have this chance to meet you. And I hope you don't mind, but there's things I need to tell somebody. I know folks have questions about me."

"You're not obliged to satisfy anybody's curiosity," Shirley said.

"Well, I'll tell you as much as anybody needs to know, and I don't care who else hears it." Emmaline leaned on the fence, watching the horses. "I come from a little place all to hell and gone in Utah. Nobody's heard of it. I was married off when I was fifteen. Not legally, not with my consent. I got away when I was sixteen. The old bastard had plenty of wives left."

"I've heard of such things, even in this day and age," Shirley said. "Good for you for getting out."

"I got by on washing dishes in diners and cafes from Idaho to Oregon and back here to Montana. No fooling with men." Emmaline glanced sideways. Shirley, knowing just what she meant, nodded.

"Along the way I picked up some education in cooking and baking, and moved up from dishwashing. Took night classes whenever I was in a college town; general education, woodworking, accounting, whatever might come in handy. Accounting class was where I met Sigri, in Bozeman."

Shirley chuckled. "I did hear the only thing Sigri got out of that class was you."

"Well, she'd already got a degree in animal science years ago. Anyway, what with needing somebody to handle the bookkeeping, and getting a taste for my cooking," Shirley let out a muffled snort of laughter, "she asked if I'd ever considered ranch life."

Close enough. Sigri'd said something more along the lines of, "Think you could put up with being a rancher's woman?"

"So I'm here. And I'm staying, as long as Sigri needs me."

Shirley put her arm right around Emmaline's shoulders. "My grandad used to say Sigri'd got no quit in her, which was why she'd make a rancher. Never was any use trying to change her mind. I reckon you'll be around as long as ever you want to."

Emmaline gave her a quick hug and looked back toward the house. The sheriff and deputies had come out, and were dragging shovels and a big pine box out of their truck.

"Shirley, parts of what I told you gave me some ideas about what might have happened with that . . . body. I'd like to tell the sheriff now, before they get to digging."

Shirley nodded and kept close beside her as they went.

Emmaline tapped the sheriff on the shoulder. "Sheriff—Frank—I might have some helpful information."

He turned, a hint of embarrassment crossing his face. "I'd sure appreciate anything you can tell me, miss. Uh, ma'am."

"Emmaline," his wife put in firmly.

"Oh. Right. Well, we're going to have a hell of a time figuring out who this guy was and what to do with him."

"First off, you might think of getting a Mormon preacher," Emmaline said. "If there's any bit of identification, wallet, initials, whatever, the genealogy experts in Salt Lake City might be able to help."

The sheriff raised an eyebrow. Even Sigri looked puzzled.

Emmaline went on quickly, "Back when I was clearing out the root cellar there was this one tin box mostly buried in the wall, so I dug it out." She bent and picked up what she'd set under the front steps that morning, not sure whether she'd show it or not. She pried off the corroded lid. Everybody strained to get a look.

"Then last night Sigri told me that there were old stories about two young boys living in the dugout, one blond, one redheaded."

Now Sigri, who hadn't said any such thing, or not exactly, raised a quizzical brow.

"I'm thinking," Emmaline said, "those weren't boys at all. They'd run away and cut off their hair, but they were girls. Or women. And then there's these, that I hadn't seen until today." She lifted out the two thin silver rings, each cut through. "Wedding bands, maybe, that they'd cut off, as well."

Frank looked dubious. Emmaline hurried right along. "Now, I'll be the first to admit it's likely just my own background talking, but I think those were two wives of a Mormon patriarch, back when that was still legal. And that . . . thing . . . caught in the cave-in in there," she jerked her head toward the house, "was either him, or somebody he'd sent to chase them down."

Sigri's arm was around her now. "Could be something to go on, Frank," she said, "but chances are we'll never know. It'll be good to get all that out of here now, anyway, the sooner the better."

It was over by mid-afternoon. The sheriff took down statements, the deputies shot pictures, and Shirley helped clean the kitchen floor after all the tramping through it. Finally Emmaline and Sigri were alone.

"How did it go in there?" Emmaline asked, when they'd sat quietly on the front steps for a little while.

"Nothing happened," Sigri said, "but everybody sure was jumpy. I didn't go all the way down till they'd dragged the bones out. Not enough room for all of us, anyway." She stared down at hands scrubbed so hard they were red. "Em, I did try to clean up your stuff down there, but there's three or four sacks of spuds you may not want to keep."

Emmaline didn't say anything. After a while Sigri turned to face her. "I've been thinking maybe . . . well, how will you feel about living here, after all this?"

"You'll stay on," Emmaline said. "You won't leave your land."

Sigri's face, for the first time Emmaline could remember, showed every one of her thirty-seven years, and more. "I'd quit the land before I'd quit you, Em."

Emmaline reached her hand out. "I think it'll be all right, now everything's been cleared away. And even if it isn't, those are my hard-raised provisions down there, and my home and heart right here." She pressed Sigri's fingers briefly to her lips. "Nothing's going to chase me away. Like your grandad said about you, I've got no quit in me, and don't you forget it!"

Her expression was fierce, but Sigri got so close, so fast, that expressions didn't matter a bit. What mattered was settled, once and for all, beyond the power of man or ghost to rend apart.

~

Sacchi Green has published stories in a hip-high stack of anthologies, including eight volumes of *Best Lesbian Erotica*, and edited more than a dozen anthologies, among them Lambda Award winners *Lesbian Cowboys* and *Wild Girls, Wild Nights,* as well as *Best Lesbian Erotica 20th Anniversary Edition, Thunder of War, Lightning of Desire: Lesbian Historical Military Erotica*, and *Through the Hourglass: Lesbian Historical Romance.* She also returns occasionally to her first love, science fiction and fantasy, sometimes under the name Connie Wilkins. http://sacchi-green.blogspot.com.

Minghun
Amy Sisson

A WHISPER OF excitement echoes through the cave, or what I think of as a cave. *She is coming, the minghun broker is coming*, I hear or perhaps feel, like soft butterfly wings brushing my face. I strain to catch a glimpse of one of the others I know to be around me, but it is difficult to see faces. A flash of sleeve, whether plain or fancy, or a pale hand laid briefly on my arm is more likely.

When she arrives, the minghun broker is far more tangible than the companions I sense around me, and her face seems familiar. She has been coming as long as I've been here, which may be months or years. It is whispered that she comes to us in her dreams, that she belongs to the world before. The others are always happy to see her because she offers something they cannot find for themselves.

So far the minghun has not sought me, and I am both sad and relieved. This time again, she glances at me with sympathy in her eyes, eyes that I know can actually see me, even when I cannot always see my own hand held up in front of my face. Then she moves on, calling softly until she finds the one she seeks.

It is Chen Yinlan this time, and the others sigh with envy. The minghun stands before Yinlan and speaks, the waves of her voice spreading like ripples in a pond.

"I bring tidings from your parents, who wish me to say: 'Beloved daughter, you died very young and did not experience the unity of marriage. You are alone in the dark and we weep to think of you longing for companionship. We have come to know that Yang Xingwu and his wife have recently lost a son as they might lose a strong young leaf to the blowing wind. They have asked for betrothal so your souls might meet; we have consented, and have chosen this auspicious day for the marriage rites and feast. Please come share this celebration with us so that we might rest, knowing your soul to be united in harmony with that of your husband.'"

The minghun pauses, and by this I am puzzled. In life such decisions do not belong to the bride, so why does the minghun ask the bride's blessing here? But ask she does, and the answer is always yes.

I do not hear Yinlan's answer, but I know she has assented because I see her spirit flare briefly into something more vital before disappearing altogether. I feel Yinlan's absence for a time, before the press of spirits closes the gap. The minghun too goes away, fading back to her world, and the cave seems more restless for a time before it settles down as much as it ever does. Always the spirits move among each other, searching and waiting and searching some more.

Some of the spirits whisper that the minghun comes less frequently now, although how they can tell I do not know. In the old days, they say, parents understood the need for minghun, but modern views discourage the practice. Only in the rural provinces do grieving parents still act on behalf of their lost children, even if they must do so surreptitiously. I do not quite know where or when I am from, a city or a village, back then or just now; all possibilities seem equally improbable, as if this place is all I have ever known.

The minghun has not yet come again since taking . . . Yinlan?—I can't quite remember her name—from us. And because there has been no sign yet of the minghun's return, I am startled to hear a voice, clear and strong, behind me. I turn to find eyes shining from the pale outline of a face. "Who are you?" the face asks.

"I am . . . I am Liu," I say. "More than that I do not know."

"It will come back to you," she says. "When you've been here a while it will start to come back."

"What is a while?" I ask. "Who are you?" But she is already gone. I think of looking for her, but instead settle down to ponder her words. I try hard to remember something of the world before, and it is tiring, but finally I am rewarded with the memory of a baby gripping my finger with surprising strength. My nephew, I realize, my brother's son, an infant already so full of life that I know he will not depart too quickly as I did. I feel the squeeze of his tiny fingers again, and I rejoice still further when I am able to envision the weave of his blanket and hear my mother's kind laughter at the rapt adoration on my face.

"Someday you—" she begins, but I am wrenched back here and I do not hear what she says. I am consumed with sorrow over the things I have lost, and even more for the things I never had and never will. I think of Ping, my friend in the village, whose beauty was incomparable. She had looked at me in a special way, I thought, or perhaps I imagined it because I wanted it to be so.

This time I feel the stranger's spirit before she speaks, and I turn to her.

"You begin to remember," she says. "I am Yan Lianghui."

"I am Qin Liu," I answer. "I am from the village Qinjalao in the Shanxi Province. I am . . . I was only fifteen when I died, of illness because there was no money for a doctor. But my family loved me and I loved them and I am not ready to be dead." Suddenly words are spilling from me as fast as my lips can form them. Lianghui listens patiently, occasionally prompting me with a question or commenting with a smile that becomes more substantial as our conversation goes on.

Time passes as Lianghui and I get to know one another, although I still do not know whether it is hours or weeks or months that unfold. She tells me delightful stories yet holds something back, something I sense she wishes to say. I am fascinated by her, and in spite of my shyness I find myself telling her of my sorrow that I will not see my nephew grow up.

"There are babies here, Liu, did you not know?" she asks gently, and suddenly I do know, and wonder how I could have been unaware. They do not cry as babies do, but I can feel them around me, waiting, puzzled, longing to be claimed by a family without knowing what a family is. I want to cry their sorrow for them, because females so young will not have parents arranging minghun for them. Indeed, some of the baby girls were almost certainly discarded by their parents.

When the minghun comes again, I am surprised, for I have been distracted by Lianghui and the thoughts she has inspired. For the first time I realize that this is a different broker, that they have not always been the same person. Like the other ones who have come, this minghun moves among us, seeking the young woman whose parents have sent her, then reciting the greetings and invitation she has been asked to convey.

The lucky young woman, Aimei, is about to consent.

"Wait, please," I say, to Aimei or the minghun or both. The minghun is surprised, and makes a sign as though to protect herself. She is accustomed to approaching spirits, not to being approached by them.

"I respectfully address you," I say, bowing my head. "Aimei has been fortunate that her parents have found a husband for her. But there are babies here, little girls whose parents cannot or will not make such arrangements. Can not Aimei take a baby with her to be part of her family?"

Lianghui speaks softly from beside me. "And perhaps a boy child as well?"

I am ashamed, for until now I have not thought of the little lost boys, who do not seem to reside with us here.

The minghun stares at us in astonishment, her lined face unbelieving. "The parents have charged me with uniting Aimei and her betrothed, who will be buried together so that they may share the afterlife. How am I to locate the remains of the little ones if their parents do not come to me?"

"Please," I say. "Is there something you can do?"

"Yes," Aimei whispers. "I should like a child to care for."

The minghun vanishes and Aimei cries out. I feel wretched, thinking that I may be responsible for preventing Aimei from finding her peace.

"Courage, Aimei," says Lianghui. "The minghun is wise and she will—"

The minghun reappears, looking more translucent than usual, perhaps from exhaustion. "I have done as you asked," she says to Aimei. "I have found a family who mourn a baby girl and approached them with this most unusual request. Your parents were frightened but your mother pleaded with your father for his consent. I must find the child." She moves off and I see small vague lights in her path. Minutes or hours later she returns to us, holding a small bundle that begins to take shape. She offers it to Aimei, who cradles it in her arms. I tentatively reach forward and place my finger in the baby's hand, and feel a ghost-tear run down my face as the baby squeezes my finger and vanishes with Aimei. My hand is surrounded by emptiness, until Lianghui squeezes it in understanding.

From that time on, Lianghui and I are seldom apart.

The next time the minghun comes, she pauses before me. I am about to ask about the children, but she bows her head and speaks my name, which I had not told her upon our last encounter.

"Qin Liu," she says. "I bring tidings from your parents, who wish me to say—"

"My parents," I whisper in wonder. "My parents . . . How long have I been here?"

"Two days, Qin Liu. You have been here two days and your parents are anxious to lay you to rest next to your betrothed, a young man also from the Shanxi Province who was snatched from his family only two weeks ago. They wish to bury you beside him so that you may have companionship in your afterlife—"

"No," I answer softly. "I have found my companionship in the afterlife." Lianghui catches her breath beside me but does not speak, and I go on. "I have found Lianghui, honored minghun, and I wish to stay here with her. We will help the girls and the women, and the babies who need a family. And if ever a time comes when no more need our help, perhaps you can lay my bones to rest with those of Lianghui."

"I will do my best," she says, and bows her head once again.

"Please," I say. "Please tell my family that I love them. Tell them—" I cannot go on, but I do not have to, for the minghun smiles at me and I know she will find the words that escape me.

Later—hours, days, months—I ask Lianghui how it can be that only two days had passed before the minghun came for me.

"It is only time, Liu, in a place that does not trouble itself with such things. It is only we who concern ourselves so." She is silent for a moment, and then she says softly, "I have waited for you for almost three hundred years."

"Did no one else come?" I ask.

"Once before, I thought one had come. But though she loved me, she left when the minghun came for her, and I cannot blame her for that." Lianghui looks at me in wonder. "But you stayed," she says.

"I stayed," I answer. I take her hand, and I feel it become more solid every moment.

~

Amy Sisson is a writer, reviewer, and librarian currently living in Houston, Texas, with her NASA spouse and a large number of ex-stray cats. Previously, her short fiction has appeared in *Strange Horizons*, *Lady Churchill's Rosebud Wristlet*, and a number of licensed *Star Trek* anthologies from Pocket Books. In January 2015, she began a project to read at least one short story every day, and blogs about her favorites at www.amysisson.com.

Wine and Magnolias
Lela E. Buis

WE GOT A late start yesterday and ran into an accident in Atlanta, so we've come in from Savannah this morning. Miller is driving the truck with our equipment, and his wife Celia and I have come separately in the car. She's a freckled redhead with brown eyes and expressive hands.

"Holly," she says, as we turn off onto the main street, "this doesn't look like a good place to have a shellfish allergy."

I look over at her. "Is that bothering you again?"

"I got a rash from the fish last week," she says.

She tugs at the hem of her shirt.

"So, order fried chicken, instead."

"What if the whole kitchen is contaminated?" she asks. "They use the same utensils, the same fat to fry the chicken."

"Go vegetarian?" I suggest.

"I'll starve," she says. "Is that the place?"

We're just north of Brunswick, Georgia, here to investigate a Bed and Breakfast hotel that's had paranormal activity. It's situated in a hole-in-the-wall community with graceful old homes still lining the streets, all framed by live oaks trailing Spanish moss. There are two or three gift shops and an art gallery, tabby ruins at the waterfront. At the docks, a line of shrimp boats provides a clue to what supports the local economy.

We've turned into the backstreets now, and I'm looking for the address. Celia's pointing to a white Victorian house at the end of the block. It's a two-story with columns, a porch, and a swing. There's a white picket fence out front. The parking area is shaded by magnolia trees, covered just now with white blossoms. There's a sign that says "Open Gates."

"That's it," I say.

I drive in under the trees and shut off the car, look around. At the end of the block, our truck turns the corner, close behind us. In another moment, Miller pulls in beside the car. He gets out and stretches, his long body uncurling like a cat from the cramped cab. He looks at the house with intense, dark eyes.

It's late summer in South Georgia, but the temperature is relatively pleasant here. It's humid, but that's always a given in the South. We're still looking at the place when a man comes walking down the street from a shop further along.

"Hey," he says. "You're the investigators, right?"

He's looking at the truck, which says "Halloran Psychic Investigations."

"Sure," says Miller. "I'm Miller Halloran and this is my sister Holly and my wife Celia."

"I'm Zak," the man says. He's taller and younger than I expected. "We bought the place about three years back," he says. "We didn't know it was haunted. This has come up really fast. You'd think it might be an attraction, but the um, manifestations have been a little too scary. It's running off our business."

"We're fairly good at recording and identifying phenomena," I say, "but you might have to find an exorcist somewhere else."

"I've found one up in Savannah," says Zak, "but she says we've got to establish what kind of phenomena we're dealing with, first. If it's something besides a ghost . . ."

"Sure," says Miller. "We can do that for you. Is there some place here to eat lunch?"

"Skip's," says Zak. "It's just around the corner at the waterfront. Do you want to stay at the B&B?"

"Not tonight," I say. "That will disturb the energy. We'll need to record it without anyone in the rooms—at least at first."

"There's another hotel just behind Skip's, then," he says.

Celia and I go off with the car and the luggage to check into the hotel, while Miller and Zak sit on the front porch of the house. They're going to do the initial interview that gives us information on the house and what's been going on. Apparently the house was built in 1876 by a timber baron who shipped his goods out from the waterfront. Zak doesn't know of any murders or other tragedies that took place there. When we get back to the B&B, Miller is done with the interview, so we head to Skip's for lunch.

Sure enough, Celia breaks out in hives within an hour after eating.

"This is awful," she says, fanning the hem of her shirt. "Miller, will you take me back to the room? I don't have any Benadryl, either. Did you see a drug store somewhere?"

We're trying to set up the equipment. He looks at me.

"I can handle it," I say. "It's all mostly carried in, so I can set it up."

"Okay," he says. "See you later."

The gear I need to set up is digital recorders and full-spectrum cameras that will record any sounds, movement, or ectoplasm that might appear. According to Zak, the manifestations include singing, moans, and screams. A couple of guests have also seen a sort of misty presence—all of this taking place at night. The B&B only has four bedrooms, three upstairs and one downstairs. In addition to that, there's a library, a living room, a dining room, a kitchen, and a utility area. I've got enough gear to cover all those and the stairs too, but it will take me all afternoon to set it up, working by myself.

There's no help for it, so I get started in the bedrooms upstairs. By five o'clock, I'm nearly done. I'm down on my knees in the downstairs bedroom, running wires for the lighting when I become aware that someone else is there.

I start, bang my head on the dresser.

"Oh, sorry," she says. "I didn't mean to startle you."

I'm just in front of a wall mirror, and my reflection sits up on its heels to have a look at her. I look like Miller in the glass, tall and dark-haired, dark-eyed. I've got on a gray tee shirt, work boots, and jeans, and my hair is up in a clip. The girl steps back, out of range of the mirror.

"That's okay," I say.

"What are you doing?" she asks.

She sits down on the bed. She's got dark skin and freckles, blondish hair and green eyes. She dressed in shorts and a plaid shirt. Her legs are long and brown and they catch my eye, the curve of the calf, the long sweep of thigh. She's a really lush, pretty girl.

"Paranormal investigation," I say.

I go back to working on the wiring, apply some duct tape to prevent a tripping hazard.

"Oh," she says. "I saw your truck outside. You're hoping to take pictures of the ghost?"

"That's right," I say.

"I'm Irina Marks," she says. "I'm here for the summer. Have you been doing this kind of work very long?"

She looks about the right age to be a college student, I think.

"About ten years," I say. "I'm Holly Halloran."

"That's so interesting," says Irina. "How did you get started with it?"

"My Uncle Joe lived in a haunted house," I say. "When we were teenagers, my brother and his girlfriend and I decided to investigate. We sort of learned the basics doing that, and once we had the equipment, we went into business together."

She looks at the cameras.

"Can you really take pictures of ghosts with those?"

"Sure," I say. "They're full spectrum, which means they go into the ultraviolet and infrared range, as well as using visible light. Ghost ectoplasm isn't like flesh and blood, but if people can see something, then the cameras can usually make it more distinct."

"Are you here by yourself?" she asks.

I explain about Celia's hives. They can actually be a sign of a serious, anaphylactic reaction, so it's something that bears watching. Miller hasn't come back, but he's not called either, so I gather he's still monitoring the situation.

"How awful," she says. "I'm glad I don't have any allergies like that."

I start putting away my pliers and tape in the toolkit.

"Are you done with the cameras?" she asks.

"Yep," I say. "It's all set up. There are monitors in the van where we can watch the video feeds later tonight. Tomorrow night one of us will stay in the house, see if it makes any difference."

"What if you find something?" she asks. "Are you a ghost . . . killer too?"

"You mean a ghost hunter?" I ask. "No, not usually."

I check my phone again, but there's nothing from Miller or Celia. I was hoping Miller would make it back pretty soon to have a look at the setup before we need to start monitoring.

"If you've got a little time," says Irina, "come sit in the living room. You can tell me about where you're from."

The living room has a Victorian style couch and overstuffed chairs in front of the fireplace. The walls are a restful green with about a foot of white crown molding at the ceiling. The floor is hardwood. There are watercolors from local artists apparently for sale on the walls.

Irina opens a cupboard in one corner and starts music, a smooth jazz.

"Do you like wine?" she asks.

"I'm not sure if Zak . . ." I start to say.

"I think I'm pretty good friends with Zak," she says. "He won't mind. He'll put it down as promotion."

I think about it.

"Okay, sure," I say.

I make myself comfortable in one of the chairs, and after a minute she comes back from the kitchen with two wine glasses and a bottle of Pinot Grigio. She serves up the wine and hands me a glass, arrays her long legs on the sofa. Her shirt pulls tight, showing off small, high breasts.

She tries out the wine and leans her head back, savoring the taste.

"This place is so romantic," she says. "Don't you like the ambience?"

"It is," I say.

She's right that it's exceptional. The bedrooms have all been beautifully furnished and it has a quaint charm while still having modern amenities. There's even a pool and a barbeque pit in the backyard.

"When I'm here, I can just see myself in one of those gorgeous Southern belle gowns," she says. "You know, the ones with the big hoop skirts and the low cut bodices? Maybe my lover would come courting, and we could sit in the porch swing outside and drink lemonade and kiss when no one is watching."

I can see the same vision. That kind of dress would suit her, I think. I have to smile.

"Do you have family here?" I ask.

"No," she says. "I came down this way on a road trip with some people from Savannah, and decided I'd like to spend the summer here—it's such a pretty little town. Since summer's nearly over, I'll be looking for a ride back soon."

"I'd think you'd be looking for more action," I say.

She looks at me straight.

"I just like quiet, out of the way places," she says. She licks her finger and runs it along the top of the glass, making it sing. "Are you from Savannah?"

"Tennessee," I say. "We've come down from Chattanooga."

"I've not been there," she says. "Would it be an interesting place to visit?"

"It's pretty," I say. "You'd like the mountains."

I've been enjoying the grassy savannahs here—the terrain at the coast is a lot different from the Appalachians.

Just then my phone sounds its tone. It's Miller.

"Hey," I say. "How's Celia?"

"Itchy," he says. "I think she'll be okay for a while, so I'm going to the chicken shack to get dinner. Do you want me to pick you up something?"

"Sure," I say. "How about some wings? I'll be there in a while."

"Are you headed off?" asks Irina.

"Yep," I say. "It's not far. I can walk."

"Watch out for the mosquitoes," she says. "You'll need to get some repellent to sit in the truck all night."

"Thanks for the wine," I say.

"Sure."

I set the glass down on the side table. She follows me out to the porch, sits in the swing and waves as I head off down the sidewalk.

Celia looks like hell, her eyes swollen almost shut.

"Dang, honey," I say. "Don't you need to see a doctor about that?"

She's sitting in bed, watching TV and scratching her belly.

"Maybe," she says. "I'm hoping the Benadryl will take care of it tonight. If it's still like this tomorrow, maybe I'll need cortisone."

Miller arrives with the wings and coleslaw then, and we dig in. We've got plenty of time before we have to start monitoring. Miller walks over and takes a look around at my setup, tweaks some of the camera settings. I can tell he's worried about Celia.

The night is uneventful, with no sign of moans, screams, or ectoplasm. It's disappointing. We knock off around dawn, head back to the hotel rooms for a few hours of sleep. At two in the afternoon, Celia still looks like hell, so Miller calls Zak and asks where to find a doctor. They head off south, looking for an ER, and leave me to check the B&B again.

The setup looks undisturbed. Zak sees me there and heads down the street.

"Anything?" he asks.

"Not last night," I say. "Still, we've got a baseline now. One of us will stay in the house tonight to see if that will provoke something."

"Okay," he says. "Listen, I've got some guests coming for the weekend. Will you be finished by then?"

I'm wondering why he didn't say something about this before. It's already Thursday. I try not to frown.

"I can't promise anything," I say. "If we don't get something tonight . . ."

"Okay," he says. He runs a hand through his hair, looks unhappy. "I've got to get back to the shop."

I've not been in the house long before Irina opens the front door.

"Holly?"

"Yeah," I call. "I'm here."

"How's your sister-in-law?" she asks.

"Not too good today," I say. I come out of the bedroom, drop onto the sofa. "Miller took her to the ER. The reaction could last a few days. If it gets any worse, it will be dangerous."

I'm starting to worry about the job now. We need the money, and if we have to leave without finishing up . . .

"I'm so sorry to hear that," says Irina. "What a way to spend the week."

She goes to the cupboard, turns on the music again.

"At least you've got some time to relax before you have to work," she says. "Would you like some wine tonight?"

I take a deep breath.

"Sure," I say.

She brings out a Riesling this time, sits on the sofa next to me. She's close enough that I can feel the heat off her body, smell the faint scent of her cologne. She props one elbow on the back of the couch, studies my face.

"Are you and your brother twins?" she asks.

I have to laugh.

"Yes," I say. "But of course we're not identical."

She laughs, too.

"You might as well be," she says. "They'll be at the ER pretty late. Why don't we have dinner here tonight? Zak has some food in the fridge that will spoil if it's not used up."

"I don't know," I say.

"Aren't you going to stay here tonight?" she asks. "You said you'd need to see if someone in the house makes a difference?"

I think about it. The plan was for Miller to stay in the house and for me or Celia to monitor, but if they're both occupied with the hives, then maybe I can take care of it myself. The monitoring is automatic once it's set up, after all. There's been no sign this ghost is dangerous, and Zak wants us out by the weekend.

"I guess I can do it by myself," I say.

"Wonderful," she says.

She reaches out, tucks a stray bit of hair behind my ear. Her touch causes a little shiver up my spine. She smiles, as if she knows it's happened.

There's leftover lasagna in the fridge. We heat it up in the oven and make salad and garlic bread. The dining room has a long table with a buffet and more of the pretty watercolors. The table is already set with crystal and linen napkins. We pull up two chairs together, have coffee in the library afterward.

It's paneled in dark wood, and the shelves of books offer information on the Golden Isles, Sapelo Island, and the local ecology. There's a nice selection of novels as well. There's another of the Victorian sofas against the windows and we sit there, enjoying the smooth music and the last of the coffee. There's thunder muttering in the distance now, a storm blowing up.

"Are you going to be finished tonight?" Irina asks.

She sitting close again, and I can smell the clean scent of her hair. She's left it down today, and it falls around her shoulders in tight, amber waves.

"It has to be tonight," I say. "Zak has some guests coming for the weekend, so we've got to have the equipment out by tomorrow afternoon."

"I'll miss you," she says. "It's been nice to have someone to talk to."

I have to laugh.

"Aren't you the one looking for a quiet place to spend the summer?"

She laughs, too.

"Listen," she says, "it's going to rain."

We can hear the first raindrops sweeping across the roof now, spatting the windows.

"Brrr," she says. She shivers, curls against me. "Don't you think it's cold in here?" she asks.

"A little bit," I say.

The difference is that I've got on jeans and a tee and she's just wearing shorts and a halter top that shows off brown, rounded shoulders and a respectable cleavage. In a moment, she leans over and kisses me on the mouth.

It's not really a surprise. I've noticed the way she's looked at me, and I've not been that shy about looking at what she's got to offer, either. I feel a rush of desire.

I lift one hand to touch her breast, feel her nipple lift and harden under the thin cloth of the halter top.

Lightning flashes in the windows. Thunder cracks. It rumbles through the house, out across the river.

Irini presses tight against me.

"Mmm," she says.

She gets up then. She takes my hand, leads me into the downstairs bedroom. Lightning flashes again, outlines her body in glowing light. We undress, wrap passionately around one another on the four-poster bed. She's golden and sweet-scented, heated already. The small, high breasts have dark nipples.

"Ahh," she says, as I slide my hand down her belly.

Thunder cracks again, rumbles into the distance. Hail clatters at the windows.

Irina buries her face in my hair, comes to climax at the height of the storm. She cuddles against me to sleep. Listening to her soft breathing beside me, I think she's the best lay I've had in a long time.

Sometime in the morning, I wake to the manifestations the guests must be complaining about. There are creaks on the stairs, something that sounds like a woman's voice. Good, I think, still half asleep. The monitors will catch it, and we'll have something to analyze in the morning. That will earn us our pay.

Later, I come fully awake by myself in the big bed. Light streams in through the windows. Irina has thrown the coverlet over me. Remembering the cameras too late, I'm thinking this needs to be a private bit of film that Miller and Celia don't see.

I have to smile at that.

I'm hoping Irina will be around for breakfast, but she's nowhere to be found this morning. Continuing my assumptions about Zak's hospitality, I help myself to coffee and muffins in the kitchen. Then I go out to check the van. I don't have time to review all the files, but I do edit out the footage of Irina and myself in the bedroom. I start to erase it, but at the last second, I decide to save it to my phone instead. Then I cut the feeds, go inside to start disassembling the gear.

I'm back at our hotel by midmorning. It seems the cortisone has nearly killed Celia's hives.

"Did you get something?" asks Miller.

"I'm sure we did," I say. "I guess someone has to be there to trigger the response."

"Great," he says. "Maybe we should head back home today, then. It'll cut down our expenses if we do the analysis at home."

We go back to the house to pick up the truck, and I'm hoping Irina will be there to say good-by. She's nowhere to be seen, though.

Damn. I didn't even get her phone number.

I'm annoyed, but I'll have to give it up. I'm going to drive the truck home, and Miller and Celia are taking the car. I take a last, hopeful look around.

"Bye, honey," I say. "It's been nice."

The house is still and silent, the porch swing only creaks a little in a slight breeze. The heavy scent of the magnolias spreads on the humid air.

I walk on out the front gate, climb into the truck cab. Irina is right that this is a nice place. Maybe I can come back again sometime as a guest.

I keep thinking about her on the trip back home, the scent of her hair, the smooth texture of her skin. Maybe I can call Zak later and ask how to get in touch with her.

There's no traffic slowdown in Atlanta this time. Back home, I have restless dreams, and it takes a lot of coffee to get me up and running on Saturday. I spend the morning going through what we've recorded, finally find a clear shot of the ghost. She was in my bedroom at the Open Gates just before dawn, a wisp of Southern belle in a hoop skirt and a low-cut bodice. She's dancing, it seems—singing. She swings her arms, throws back her curly head.

It's Irina.

I close my eyes, feel the touch of her hands again, the soft brush of her lips. Whether or not I see her again, she's going to haunt me now.

~

Lela E. Buis is an artist, author, and poet. She grew up in East Tennessee and lived for a long time in Florida. She began writing as a child and leans toward genre fiction, having published mainly science fiction, fantasy stories, and poetry. When she's not painting or writing, she looks after four barn cats and a part-time dog.

Scratch of the Spectre
Lee Altomaro

WHAT WAS THAT noise? It crept into her sleep and pried her out of dreams. Something about it didn't sound right. Like forced water crackling through holes laced with static, not the kind of soothing sound heard with the movement of running water. A scratch. As if the hand of a malevolent god had circumscribed the heavens and allowed the first glints of Armageddon to slip into her consciousness. A blight, an imperfection upon her highest level of self-awareness. A waterfall made of scissors and nails and aluminium screening. All the jagged courses of wonder heaving themselves into a pile of nothing more than broken ceramic dreams. How to know, if this was a dream, why did the veil feel so thin, like crepe paper?

She thought about finding her legs and moving position, but there was something taut around her limbs that made moving impossible. It felt like rope. Maybe she had been kidnapped and was down in some dark cellar, tied up and awaiting God knows what.

It happened when everything seemed to be going so well, or at least as well as could be expected. She had a good job, a few good friends, and had become closer to her family in recent months, so it wasn't as though she had to feel all alone in the world.

Family support notwithstanding, the last three years had been challenging, having lost her lover of sixteen years to a disease so rare it only happened to one of out every half a million people. She and Maggie had done everything together, and were closer to each other than most people were after a lifetime, so when the doctor gave them the prognosis, it was as if the world had collapsed in on them.

It was a lot of work, but somehow she managed to stay above water. Still, she had not really been able to let go—her mind stretched out upon so many long, lonely days since the day of the funeral, as if she was living in a nuclear winter. The trouble started one day when she was preparing breakfast, a premonition. The coffee was a little bitter, she was running a little late, but a pause, to hear something that hid behind the walls, behind the newness of the awakening day. A scratch. The sun was out but the colors of the world were all wrong. The very air inside and out of her seemed to have no life. The sound that should have been there either way was absent, and the footfalls of past platitudes, even they were not within echo.

How many times before had she heard this absence, felt this absence, even when Maggie was alive? How many cruel manifestations of a nothingness attained? A chasm not identified? Was it a missing link? Was she born without the enviable piece of armor that seemed to make most people appear to be fluid and blissfully unaware? Why was it so difficult for her to be at peace? Not to say that there weren't plenty of times in her body, whole, and limitless, when she could honestly say, that the world was painted as pure as the sun at birth, as bright as the snow on Christmas day, and as soft as a mother's embrace.

But that noise. The absence of the links that bound the hand, the legs, the head, the arms. As if on the day they handed out instructions, she had instead broached the event horizon. A black hole, spreading out from center, swallowing the illumination of her given birthright. It was as if a force unknown was trying to claw its way inside.

On that morning, on the way to work, to the place where among the bodies, sitting mostly, the tasks were laid out for her. The purpose was defined. That always felt right. Working. She didn't have to question her purpose. She could feel at peace there. But all that space when she stepped back out into the day. It should have felt light, but it felt heavy. All that possibility, all that not knowing. She could go here or there, under or above.

She could go nowhere or everywhere, and who would know the difference?

The roads all led to the same place, the same now and again. Endless and yet short in stature. The texture sometimes changed. The vibrations sometimes changed. The land was always there, belying ancient wisdom. Is that what had happened? Had she stepped outside and never stepped back in? For now everything she was experiencing was just ruminations of the mind. The taut strappings were still holding, not allowing her to see, to move, to breathe.

She could only fathom a feeling inside her, in which she knew there was something there that was alive but buried. The growing sense that something wasn't quite right. Something she had known, something she used to know. It was there if she could only see it. But how could she see something if her head wouldn't move, couldn't move? Tracing her line of vision only allowed for a peek into more black, more nothing. Except for the palpable absence of light, she felt nothing save panic.

There was a vibration. It echoed across a thousand walls, it beckoned her toward highways and fast food joints and empty spaces. It hearkened outward among the lost. It had no direction but it was everywhere. It was always there. It had always been there. Sometimes she forgot about it and didn't feel it for several days.

But today was not one of those days. Today was going to be a day of reckoning. She could feel it in her bones. She knew that as sure as she knew that something terrible must have happened to her. Smashing, wrenching visions of no rest. Journeys taken deep into the night and lingering past dawn. What was that sound? Had she taken a wrong turn? The spaces were all around, the trees had been covering for her. Was it raining? Had she fallen asleep in some strange place?

Maybe she had been knocked unconscious, was becoming delirious, could now be uninhibited, free to express anything, everything, inner sensors beginning to lose their hold. After all, the mind was always free to create its own pathways of illusion. She could be anywhere.

Although her mind could wander without censorship, the same couldn't be said for her body. That corporeal entity was, she realized now without a doubt, gravely incapacitated. Paralyzed, with fear, or due to bodily resistance, she couldn't determine which. Either one could cause the same seemingly hopeless situation. Either one could incite a person to pull down, deep into the depths of their most elusive trepidations and fears. Yet, situations like these could also allow for the realization of that extraordinary strength that a person could only tap into when the going got rough.

And this going was rough. That much she knew. She had been through how many challenges like this before, too many to count. Days when it was all she could do to try and maintain a grasp on her mind; to try and hold on to even just a small thread of sanity that could connect her to the world, that which was her most basic self. But some days it seemed even that was too much to ask for. Some days the smallest perceived indignity, the smallest disappointment, or the most ludicrous of doubts, could take her mind hostage and deliver her to the proverbial nuthouse.

Nothing had to actually happen, nothing had to actually change. The changes all occurred within her mind, they were not actually taking place in the world. No one else could see them. Most people didn't even notice them. It all seemed surreal. Yet the searing heat of summer and the unforgiving chill of winter, those things still felt real enough to touch, and because she felt them, she knew that she was alive.

In a room, in a house, an automobile, a workplace, in those and in all places, so arbitrarily put into her space. She walked through them. But it was as if they were placed, as if someone or something else had put those things there. Put them there for her to live in, to work in, to think in, to wonder in, to love in, and to grieve in. Which one of those arbitrary places her body was currently inhabiting she didn't know.

She was hungry. Springing from the depths of her abdomen. Her body ached, it asked, it pleaded, it insisted. It wouldn't take no for an answer. It was pure hell, yet the unambiguity of that hunger, that desire, was in a strange way, comforting. It forced her to become single-minded. It forced her to focus on that one single thing. And that one single thing was going to require her to find a way to obtain the strength and nourishment she needed to try and get out of her current situation.

But how could she feed herself without the use of her hands, her limbs, her ability to move? How would she know where to begin, if she didn't even know where she was starting from? She must think, try to remember. There was a sound, like a scratch, it opened up into a sky full of possibilities; though seemingly sinister, it might help her to get through this thing, if only from the inside out. It seemed like so much time had passed, eons spent wandering through an abyss, a chasm.

And then as if from a thousand abbreviated miles away, another sound now. Heavier than a scratch. A tear. No, not a tear. A rip, like fabric being seared and laboriously pulled away from a long encapsulated tomb, a catacomb, her catacomb, the whereabouts of which were unknown to her or to anyone. What could possibly be the perpetrator of this auditory illusion?

The ripping sound became courser, closer, heavier, and it spoke of great urgency. And with the tearing, the slowly dawning realization that she was beginning to feel the sensation of movement. Her legs, her arms. Whatever it had been, the bindings that had held her captive for so long, were beginning to loosen. She heard the sound of voices, they seemed to be coming from close by, it sounded like someone was saying, "No one could have survived this."

She let go of a heated breath, it gushed out of her in an exultant gasp, and was immediately replaced by a cold rush of air that gloriously plunged into the space that her breath had occupied just moments before. She inhaled, she reached, and the blackness began to fade into light.

Then she saw it. A shadow-shape painfully silhouetted bright against the night sky. A ghostly presence that had come to liberate her. She knew that shape, had been intimate with that shape. It was beckoning to her. Maggie. She took hold of her hand. Joined together now, they were cast out from the wreckage and absconded swiftly up into the moonless sky, where they were placed, forever. Two bright stars shining down on Mother Earth.

~

Deborah Schmidel is the author of poetry, short stories, and memoir, writing under the pen name of Lee Altomaro, and draws her material from life experiences and is particularly interested in psychological suspense. She attended Cabrillo College, Norwalk Community College, and UCONN, as well as a year at Monterey College of Law. She holds an Associate Degree in Liberal Arts and is currently working toward a bachelor's degree in English. Deborah has written and choreographed lay services for the Unitarian Society in Stamford, Connecticut including "Notes in a Life" and "Everything Happens for a Reason." She lives and works in Fairfield County, Connecticut, sometimes known as the sixth borough of New York City.

Endurance
Elaine Burnes

CAPTAIN KATE RANDALL lies in a fetal curl, shivering. Voices chatter, yell, complain, plead. Clammy fingers pull at her. Sounds, cries, fill her small quarters. Ghostly forms swirl, shrieking. Wailing. The stuff of banshees. Are they in the room or inside her head? She can't tell. They deserve her attention. It's her fault they are here. No, not entirely. She wasn't responsible for whatever tossed their ships through space like bits of tissue down a toilet drain.

How long has it been? A couple of months? Since she woke to the pounding, the loss of gravity, to formerly settled objects flying through the air. Go back earlier, to her last happy moment. When she'd sat in the observation lounge mentally flirting with Natalie, the expedition leader giving a talk about Saturn, visible overhead through the panoramic observation dome.

As Natalie pointed out Saturn's E ring, and how it formed from material spewing off the second-largest moon, Enceladus, Kate finished her wine and slipped away. This would be a good time for rounds, while the guests were busy ogling Saturn and munching Martian cheeses. She always began on the lowest deck, in the engineering suite overseen by Edward. Never Ed or Eddie. "My mother named me Edward," he'd told her when they'd met and he refused her handshake. Nothing personal, Marc, her first officer, had warned her ahead of time. Autism made him more comfortable around the powerful engines of a spaceship than the warm embrace of a human. And no one could finesse the Recyc-All like Edward.

"Everything shipshape, Chief?" she asked.

"Yes, Captain," he replied, not making eye contact. "You know that. That's my job."

She smiled. "Yes, I do. And you do it better than anyone. Carry on."

"Captain." Said with a nod. The closest he could come to a thank you or good night.

On the galley deck, she refrained from snitching a snack. The staff were busy cleaning up and prepping for breakfast. She caught the eye of Miriam, the executive chef. "I can dry if you want."

Miriam laughed. "Go on. You're useless here and you know it."

Between stops, as she roamed the hallways, she engaged her augmented reality chip and whispered, "Tara." A woman appeared, visible only to Kate. Not suited for space, she wore casual clothes, like she did back when they shared a home on those brief leaves between missions. As they walked, Kate mentally chatted, told her about her day, how at dinner Mr. Singh grabbed her knee. Tara didn't say anything, her quiet presence was all Kate needed.

Before entering the bridge, Kate blinked Tara off. Lucy sat at con. With *Endurance* in stationary orbit, just two other bridge crew monitored systems.

"It's a beautiful night," Kate said as she took the first officer's seat next to Lucy.

"It's always night, Captain," Lucy responded with a sideways glance and grin. It was an old joke between them. "Should I relinquish con?"

"Just visiting. Carry on." Kate fingered the ring on Lucy's left hand. "Nice rock. When did that happen?"

Her second officer blushed, and her wide smile warmed Kate. *Oh, to feel that again.*

"When we were loading."

Kate's eyebrows rose in question.

"Rob said he had planned it for a romantic Christmas Eve, but decided he couldn't wait." She fingered the small diamond. "It feels funny. Kind of in the way."

"You'll get used to it."

They chatted for a few minutes about wedding plans and honeymoons. Then Kate said goodnight and turned in. She changed into a fresh suit and put the old one in the Recyc-All. The downside of space travel was not being able to sleep nude, to feel the soft sheets. Her mind returned to Natalie. All that talk of weddings. Natalie was as off limits as Kate. One married, the other resolved.

KATE WOKE TO a brilliant flash filling the cabin and the pressure of the snug bedding that kept her from crashing into the ceiling. Her lamp, her helmet, everything not locked down spun and swirled like so many leaves in a strong wind. A shriek of metal tearing, glass shattering. How long did it last? A minute? Less? Like that earthquake when she was a kid, but worse. Even before things settled, alarms sounded. The staccato shrill warning of hull breaches. Red lights flashed. Life support systems failing. Instinctively she activated her suit, sealing her in, applying pressure against the impending void. She squirmed out of the bedding, locked tight as a safety measure for just such circumstances, and floated. It took maybe a minute to find her helmet, flung out of its compartment next to the bed and wedged under the desk chair. Snapped into place, she bit the com tab. "Captain to the bridge. Lucy, what's going on?"

No reply.

"Captain to engineering. Respond, Chief."

Nothing.

"Captain to sick bay! Activate!"

While she spoke, Kate floated, bouncing off walls and furniture, making her way to the door leading to the bridge. It didn't respond from the control panel. She reached for the manual release, hesitating only a moment from what might lie beyond.

"Sick bay to the Captain," Dr. Amos replied, calm. "Do you have an emergency?"

"Sure sounds like it from the alarms I'm hearing. What's going on?"

"You activated me," the doctor said. "I'm downloading status updates now."

"Go to Code Red, and remain active until I release the order. Assist all injured."

"Acknowledged."

Kate braced her feet against the wall and heaved on the door. It slid in a stutter, its alignment off. Her training had prepared her for this, whatever this would turn out to be. But knowing a hundred tourists were relying on her, none of them trained, gave her pause as she pushed through to the bridge.

Two crew members floated, unconscious. Lucy, masked as a helmeted form, flew about, corralling her helpless colleagues, activating suits, snapping helmets into place, collecting loose equipment. Kate didn't think to look out the window, just joined the frantic effort.

Once the bridge was secured, Kate opened a shipwide com line. "This is Captain Randall—"

What should she say? Normal emergency procedure required reporting to muster stations, but what if those areas were compromised? She took a deep breath and let it out slowly, calming herself.

"This is Captain Randall," she repeated. "All crew, Code Red. All passengers, activate your suits and attach your helmets as we practiced. If you are in a safe place, remain there." *And if not?* "Wait for a crewmember to assess your situation. Please remain calm. Although this is not a drill, we will regain control shortly. If you have a medical emergency, the Advanced Medical Officer System has been activated and is available to respond."

Over the next hours, Kate accounted for her crew and passengers, gave orders, followed requests from engineering, sealed off damaged compartments, initiated diagnostics, and sent out an SOS. Deck by deck, the crew identified damage and initiated repairs. To her relief, *Endurance* lived up to its name.

It wasn't until the next day that Kate and her first officer entered the airlock to the domed observation deck. Sightseeing was off the itinerary for now. The emergency hatches had slammed shut automatically.

Kate needed a ground truth observation of what her navigation officer insisted must be a damaged sensor that left them unable to mark their location in space. Their last known position had been orbiting Saturn. That should be easy to check, but the smaller windows hadn't produced the planet or its rings.

Kate tethered herself to what had been the floor of the lounge but was now the outer hull and floated into open space. Walls rose to waist height, and where glass and frames would take over to allow an almost unfettered view, nothing remained. Nothing between her and infinity. And no Saturn.

Kate stared toward three suns where only one should be shining. She tapped Marc on the shoulder and directed his attention. "What the hell is that?"

A long pause. "It ain't our sun, that's for sure."

KATE ASSEMBLED HER senior staff. Natalie, with a master's in astronomy, was the closest Kate had to a science officer, so she tasked her with figuring out what happened. Could the shock that hit the ship have been the sun splitting into three? Ridiculous. Stars don't do that. Why were the sensors out of whack?

"So where are we?" Kate had already read Natalie's report. She wanted to hear it from her.

Natalie cleared her throat. Her voice shook. "Two of those stars are Alpha Centauri A and B, with Proxima over to the side." She pointed needlessly at the photo in her presentation.

The room was quiet while this sank in.

"But I saw Orion out there," said Sharyn, the hotel manager. She would bear the brunt of easing the guests' growing anxiety.

"The angle is wrong," Edward muttered. "The angle is wrong."

"Both true," Natalie said. She clicked to the next photo. "See Cassiopeia over there? Look just to the left. That star there." Natalie pointed to a tiny speck of light. "That's our sun."

Gasps, right on cue. Murmurs rose to a chatter.

Kate tapped her coffee mug on the table. "We all remember our high school astronomy, right?" she said in an even tone. She leveled her gaze on Natalie. "Roughly, four light years, correct?"

She nodded nervously.

Kate turned to Lucy. "Our maximum speed is . . . what?" She knew the answer. She knew Lucy knew she knew the answer. But it needed to be said, and she wanted everyone participating.

"A million miles per hour."

"Anyone care to do the math?"

Silence.

"I didn't think so. I'll do it for you. We're talking a good three thousand years."

Kate watched the expressions on her crew. They'd worked together for five years, ferrying tourists around the solar system, a fine-tuned machine, with never so much as a space-sick passenger, never mind a major malfunction or crisis. Lucy looked straight ahead, stricken, no doubt thinking of Rob. Marc closed his eyes and let out a breath. She'd come to rely on him for so much—advisor, friend, almost a brother. Miriam covered her face with her hands. She had family back on Earth. She didn't need this. None of them did.

"How is that possible?" Sharyn said. Her voice hollow and thin.

"Not possible," Edward muttered,shaking his head.

Kate didn't allow herself to think about home. This wasn't the time for grieving. She stood and crossed her arms. Her staff needed reassurance. "Something pushed us four light years in the time it takes the San Andreas fault to shift six feet. Maybe we can figure out how it can get us back."

HERE'S WHAT WE know. Kate replayed the mental exercise each night as she fell into bed—gravity fully restored. The ship survived whatever this was well. The self-repair programs were making progress. A third of the hull breaches were sealed. The dome, made of self-replicating material like all of *Endurance*, was regrowing and in another week would be safe for passengers to enter. But should they? What will they think when they see no Saturn, no sun, three suns?

Back to what we know. No one died. Medical nanobots in the injured activated automatically as programmed, and bones were healing, cuts closing. All were accounted for. But passengers were asking questions. Questions without answers. Why can't we call home? Why hasn't a rescue vehicle shown up? When will we get back to port?

THEN MARC GAVE her news. "There's a ship out there, Captain. Issuing a Mayday."

We're not alone. A cruise ship. Kate had seen it when they'd left Mars. The glittery *Aphrodite* had nineteen decks and eight thousand passengers. *Endurance*, with five decks and a hundred passengers, could fit in its botanical garden. Large cruise ships are built to provide a stunning entertainment experience. The Jupiter-class *Aphrodite* was a pleasure palace in every sense of the phrase. Large viewing windows, open interior space for waterfalls, zip lines, roller coasters, bars, restaurants. Kate wondered why anyone would bother to travel through space on these behemoths when they could do the same stuff on Earth with much less risk.

Kate ordered *Endurance* moved to within visual range. Maybe we can help each other, she thought.

Once she got a good look at the *Aphrodite*, however, everything that had been looking up went south. Built only for space travel, ships this size couldn't withstand the stresses of launch or reentry, never mind whatever had hit it and *Endurance*. Half the ship was simply missing.

A well-trained officer is schooled in the art of compartmentalization. Deal with what you can in the moment. In this moment, Kate ordered a rescue mission. Not rescue, exactly, since there was no way eight thousand souls could fit on *Endurance*, assuming all had survived, and looking at it, that seemed unlikely. One of *Endurance*'s small lifepods, with Lucy piloting and Kate as co-pilot, circled the ship, assessing damage, looking for signs of life. Marc hadn't wanted her to go. What if something happened to her? He was right, of course. Kate, more than anyone, knew that. But she'd also learned the hard way that no one else could take on this responsibility. Triaging injured was a mundane task compared to what awaited her.

A cloud of debris made navigating arduous. All decks were exposed, layered like a cake with a large center opening that in this case did not hold frosting or jam. Just a jam of a different sort. If the ship had any self-sealing capabilities, whatever hit her did too much damage too fast for them to close off. Conduits, wiring, and insulation hung shredded. The few bodies that floated past were in pajamas or nude. No one seemed to have been wearing a suit. *They aren't that uncomfortable. Did the company even provide them?*

All that luxury came with a price, and the *Aphrodite* was a fragile egg now cracked open and spilling its guts. A Humpty Dumpty that was not going back together again.

Dread washed through Kate. She would have to decide what to do for any survivors. Could they fit on board *Endurance*? What if there were too many? Whom do you save? She adored her crew, but they were not survivalists. Not that she expected to find needed expertise on the *Aphrodite*. Any astrobiologists in the house? How about a propulsion physicist? Anyone know how to open a wormhole?

Lucy steered the small craft toward the bridge. If it survived, there might be command staff alive. Kate and Lucy peered through the windows as they floated along the wide bridge.

Missing panes signaled a sad reality. Then they saw a figure, helmeted, suited, strapped into the command seat.

"*Endurance* to *Aphrodite*," Kate said into her mic.

"*Aphrodite* here," a faint voice gasped, adrenaline worn off, exhaustion remaining.

"What is your status?"

"Status? We're fucked."

Lucy skillfully docked onto the roof of *Aphrodite*'s bridge. The port view revealed an empty swimming pool, its protective dome gone. Thomas Philbrick, the third officer, came aboard. Nearly catatonic with trauma, he could barely speak. He told a story Kate knew. The captain had been sleeping, as had Kate, when something hit the ship or something happened to the ship. He wasn't clear. It was the night shift, skeleton crew. They were parked below Saturn's rings so they could illuminate the observation lounges where parties were in full swing. A Solar System Soirée.

Thomas hadn't left the bridge since he'd made a minor exploration of the surrounding areas. The captain was gone, his quarters, with its domed ceiling, voided to space. There might be people alive. He could feel vibrations through the superstructure. Some banging. Not random like a swinging bolt. Frantic. Fading.

First tough decision. Ask Thomas to return to *Aphrodite*, or bring him aboard *Endurance*?

"I can't make you go back, but you are the senior surviving officer," she said in a gentle tone.

He looked stricken. "What am I supposed to do there?"

Kate didn't know him. Had no idea of his background or training. "Let's get you rested and fed. We have a lot of decisions to make."

The third officer nodded, mute.

Back on *Endurance*, Kate called her senior staff together to discuss options. Follow-up reconnaissance determined there were approximately 600 souls alive, relatively safe in interior rooms that didn't breach. Mostly passengers, but also a few crew members. Housekeeping, galley staff, engineering. Food lockers survived, but there was no way to distribute it, too many voids to cross.

Kate operated on autopilot as she doled out assignments. Over the next week *Endurance* teams located a dozen viable lifepods, filled them with food, and loaded survivors onto them, managing to assign one crew member to each. Thomas Philbrick reluctantly took command.

Meanwhile, repairs to *Endurance* continued. At first her passengers were understanding. Clearly a bigger emergency lay off the starboard side. Those with useful skills, like engineers, were asked to help. Most did. What she really needed were doctors, nurses, and therapists, all professions that had died out with the rise of AI service suppliers and medical nanobots injected into children like vaccines in the past. "Where's a damn medic when you need one?" Kate grumbled.

By day, or by the twenty-two hour shifts Kate pulled, she operated smoothly, controlling what she could. The rest had to wait. Like the growing complaints among her passengers, asking why no one was coming to their rescue. She didn't hide the fact of the three suns from them. The observation deck wasn't open yet, but there were windows. Did they not want to see what was out there?

If *Endurance* had encountered a wormhole, she survived, but barely. A prototype military vessel never pressed into actual combat, the ship was kitted out for exploration. But not this kind. Exploration of the already known, not this unknown.

The *Endurance* crew salvaged everything they could from *Aphrodite*. Fuel, spare parts, Recyc-Alls. Not the roulette wheel, although they might as well have, given their chances.

As the fresh food ran out, Edward programmed the Recyc-Alls to make S rations. Miriam grumbled privately, but to the guests joked with a shrug, "It tastes like chicken."

No repairs to *Aphrodite* were possible, little living space remained, the lifepods were full but not crammed. *What next?*

The question wrapped Kate in a shroud. She turned to Tara, consulting her former commander in the privacy of her quarters. Dr. Amos would not be amused to hear her seeking advice from a figment of her imagination.

"You know what you have to do," Tara said.

"Last resort," Kate replied. The memory stabbed her. "Could you try to be more helpful?"

"What would Tara do? Is that what you want to know?"

"I didn't sign up for this."

"You know what—"

Kate turned her off. The problem with augmented reality was the infuriating lack of imagination. Projecting your own thoughts into the image of someone else wasn't much use.

Kate considered. The pods were designed to support life for a month, the time it would take for rescuers to come from Mars or Earth to Saturn or elsewhere in the solar system. That solar system. Not this one. The pods were no sturdier than *Aphrodite* and not intended for long journeys or harsh conditions.

Natalie reassured Kate that there were bound to be planets in the area, likely resource rich, maybe habitable. Kate discussed the options with her staff.

"We can't drag these people along like ducklings," she said. "There isn't enough fuel for that if we wanted to."

The unspoken question tightened with each passing hour. Stay or leave? Look for help or watch each other die?

Kate composed her message to the *Aphrodite* survivors carefully. "We are not abandoning you," she stressed. "We are going for help since help doesn't seem inclined to come to us. We'll be back. One month. We'll be back."

Earth's solar system could be transited in a month. Kate chose to overlook the paucity of habitable planets back home. "We only need one."

After she gave the order to depart, she disconnected the com link to the pods, so she couldn't hear their pleas.

Natalie used the ship's rudimentary telescope to find objects big enough to be planets or at least moons, and Lucy plotted the most efficient route past them. Each turned out to be nothing but rock or gas or gas or rock. Life might be possible with twenty years of ferrying supplies and building habitats, as had been done on Mars. Nothing to help 700 survive the rest of their lives or get back home.

Dejected didn't even begin to describe Kate's mood as *Endurance* finished its month-long circuit of the Alphas and Proxy, as they came to call the three stars.

"We've only checked a fraction of the possible candidates," Natalie said, whether to reassure or complain, it wasn't clear.

"We have to go back," Kate said.

"And do what?"

"I promised."

APHRODITE'S PODS HAD been left docked end to end, creating a long train. As they came into view, Kate saw only six. Where were the rest?

"This is *Endurance*. Can you read me?"

A pause. A crackle. Silence.

She led a team to check them out. Again, Marc protested. Again she ignored him.

At the Air Force Academy, Kate had studied how people respond in a crisis. The evidence showed that a strong leader increased the likelihood of survival. She'd left these people with no one capable in charge. It had been too much to ask of Third Officer Philbrick. The result was predictable. The six remaining pods were empty of humans but filled with clues to what happened. Bloody suits, smashed helmets, trashed equipment. In the last one they searched, a woman named Georgie left recordings. Kate sent her team back to *Endurance*'s pod and watched the messages alone.

It had taken just two weeks for civilization to shatter. Factions formed, groups disagreed on what to do. Some wanted to go back to the *Aphrodite*, others wanted to head back to Earth.

Except they had no idea where that was, and although they'd been told how far, despair made them forget or disbelieve.

In the background, over the course of the daily recordings, arguing changed to panic, screams to moans. To silence. Equipment broke down, not designed for actual survival circumstances, meant only for a few hours floating. Georgie held up a broken switch. "This is plastic, for god's sake." Early in the month, she still managed fury. "Let this be a record that I hold Galaxy Cruises responsible. And *Endurance*. They abandoned us. Captain Randall refused to let any of us on board. Not even the children."

Especially not the children. Kate needed adults. *Space is no place for children.*

Georgie's last message, "Bryan, if this ever reaches you. I'm so sorry. I do love you. This was a stupid idea and you were right. I'm so, so sorry."

Kate couldn't wipe the tears that streamed behind the safety shield of her helmet. She rode back to *Endurance* in silence then called her senior staff together. She asked for volunteers among the passengers and sorted teams. "Collect significant personal items from each stateroom. Download everything possible from their computers."

Marc pulled her aside to question her judgment.

"These people had homes, loved ones, families," Kate said. "We can't bring their bodies back, so we have to let their loved ones know what happened."

"We're three fucking thousand years from home! And we don't have the room."

"One small storage room for solid items. Recordings, photos, passports, all can be downloaded. Do it."

After everything had been retrieved, Kate spent her evenings watching video, listening to diaries. Security cameras captured the event itself. Valuable footage in one sense. Possibly helpful in an investigation, if there ever could be one.

It was as though pulling the belongings and computer files

onto *Endurance* brought the people aboard as well. That comforted Kate. At first.

She didn't believe in ghosts. She thought she was hallucinating from the stress with the first fleeting images. A little girl running through hallways in her pajamas. An old man in a wheelchair. Brief. She'd blink, and they'd be gone.

Then she heard voices. She often thought they were real. She'd turn and say, "What?" but there would be no one there. Or Marc would look at her funny and repeat what he'd just said. Indistinct, quiet, just murmurs. Then one day, the old man, instead of sitting quietly by the dining room window, turned to Kate and shouted, "Why did you leave us to die?" Horribly angry. Kate froze. Miriam asked her if she was okay. They'd been talking. Of course Kate didn't tell her what she saw.

At night, she'd hear party music, laughter, clinking glasses. She'd be alone in her bed. Could they be partying on the bridge? After several nights of this, it changed. Amid the music, there came a terrible crashing, a bright light, then screams. Horrible screams, of people being ripped apart like Kate had seen on the security camera footage. The whole ship ripped in pieces, shredded like paper.

She woke up drenched in sweat. That messed with the suit's sensors, alerting Dr. Amos. He checked her out, wondered if she had the flu. Dr. Amos, being artificial, was easy to confess to, so Kate told him what was going on. He agreed it was probably stress and activated her antidepressant bots. Then sedative bots so she could sleep. Soon she felt like how she imagined a bot felt. Nothing. She hacked into the doctor's computer and deactivated them. Better to feel rotten than nothing.

The visions and sounds worsened. Next she felt them touching her. Pulling at her. She wasn't sleeping, hardly eating. She went to bed with a massive headache and then couldn't make herself get up again. They entered her quarters like a jury, judge, and prosecutor, hovering, demanding, accusing. Dereliction of duty, abandonment, murder.

CAPTAIN KATE RANDALL lies in a fetal curl. Ghostly forms swirl, shrieking. Marc is among them.

Did I kill him too?

"Captain, are you all right? Should I call the doctor?" His voice fades into the background accusations.

A woman comes into view. Not a ghost. She can tell the difference now. The movies got that right. Ghosts are less detailed. Natalie.

"What can I do for you?" Kate says, pretending to sound normal.

"You may not have noticed, what with being holed up in your quarters for the last three days, but this ship needs a captain and that would be you."

"I'm not a real captain. I ferry tourists around the solar system."

"Your conduct since this emergency and your military service record would seem to indicate otherwise. You were a member of the elite Pulsar Force, correct?"

"How do you know that?"

"Ship's records, Captain. You aren't the only one collecting things. I know what happened on Enceladus."

Enceladus?

Tara appears beside Natalie, dim, ghostly. Kate hadn't called her up. "You know what you have to do, Kate."

"What you *made* me do? No way." Kate pulls the blanket over her head.

"They only think they know what happened. You know the truth."

"The truth? That you sacrificed yourself and the entire team to save me?"

"Is that what you think?"

"You never should have gone down to that moon. I should have gone. For that matter, no one needed to go. The New Soviets had beaten us to Enceladus. You knew I'd be stranded."

"But alive."

"You knew you wouldn't make it back."

"No, I didn't know that."

Kate's love for Tara had blinded her. The poorly planned expedition left Kate alone in the moon's orbit. Supplies exhausted, no way to get back. Then the landing pod returned.

"Captain!"

Kate yanks the blanket down and focuses on Natalie. "You have no idea what happened on Enceladus."

"I know that your commander and crewmates died on the moon, stranding you. That the pod returned on autopilot and you used it to make enough fuel to get back."

"Fool. Believing that. Tell her the truth, Kate."

Kate scowls at Tara. The truth. That the reason the crew's bodies were never found on the moon wasn't because of the terrible storm but because half the team died before getting there, and Tara refused to turn back. She went to the moon alone and died in the pod. When it returned to the orbiter, Kate, stunned, listened to Tara's final message. "You know what you have to do."

Kate dismantled the pod and filled the Recyc-All to make S rations. Only then did she put Tara's body in. That gave her the fuel she needed to get within range of rescue. She left that out of the report. After Enceladus, she quit Pulsar Force and became a tour-ship captain and vowed she'd never again get involved with anyone she worked with or venture into harm's way.

"Captain!" Natalie's shaking her now. "We need you to decide what to do. Do we go home or look for a planet to stay on?"

"This isn't a starship."

"So make do. I did. I've modified the telescope to look for planets capable of life."

"You did? Can you build a safe wormhole and get us back?"

"Not yet."

"But you will."

"I'll try. If you will."

Kate struggles to sit up, weak. The headache has moved into the rest of her body. She looks up to see Tara standing amid the crowd of *Aphrodite* passengers, all watching her expectantly.

"You know what you have to do."

"Fuck you, Tara."

"Captain?"

Kate looks from Natalie to Marc to the ghosts.

Something got us here, so something can get us back.

"I'll do it for them."

Natalie follows her gaze. "There's no one there."

"Oh, yes there is."

~

Elaine Burnes grew up and lives in Massachusetts. After twenty years working and writing for a variety of environmental nonprofits, she wearied of reality and turned to writing fiction in her spare time, publishing her first story in 2010. Since then, she has had several more stories published in *Wicked Things* (Ylva, 2014), *Best Lesbian Romance 2011* (Cleis Press), and online in *Read These Lips Take 5*, and *Khimairal Ink*. These stores are collected in *A Perfect Life and Other Stories* (GusGus Press, 2016). Her first novel, *Wishbone* (Bedazzled Ink, 2015) received a 2016 Golden Crown Literary Society Award for Dramatic/General Fiction.

Lucky Strike
L.K. Early

LOOKING BACK, I can't say how long I floated facedown in those still, dark waters. A couple of minutes? A couple of hours? A whole lifetime? I have the vaguest recollection of seeing the light of the campfire near the shore, of hearing my fellow campers sing their campfire songs, but with my mouth full of muddy water, there was no way to call for help.

And so I drifted, alone—well, not completely.

But wait, let me back up. Let me try to tell it from the beginning.

Camp Firefly was little more than a handful of decrepit cabins in a clearing near a small mountain lake. There was one campfire ring and five parking spaces, a cafeteria and some picnic tables. My parents insisted I go there to make friends, but until that night I had succeeded in making none.

After dinner I snuck away from the cafeteria and headed down to the lake to be alone. I sat in the damp grass and poked idly at the mud with the end of a twig.

That night the moon was only a sliver of gold in the twilight. Crickets chirped and every now and then a fish popped up to eat the water bugs on the surface of the lake, breaking the reflection of the moon into a million refractions of itself. But then things became calm and the water became still and the moon was just the moon again.

I tallied out the days with my twig in the mud.

One, two. Two days ago Madison Queen tricked me into kissing her in front of the other girls, just to prove that I was a lesbian.

One, two, three. Three more weeks until I could go home.

Next I counted out the cuts and bruises on my body. *One,*

two . . . thirteen. The last run-in with Madison had been the worst so far, leaving me with a bloody nose and a bruised eye that I had a hard time explaining to the camp counselor.

The next time she will kill you.

The thought was so clear, so decisive, that it sent a shiver right through me. I paused and glanced around, but I saw only trees and shadows.

I shook my head and resumed my tally marks.

No sooner had I shoved the twig into the mud did I strike something just below the surface. I thought for a moment that it was a leaf or a turtle's nest, but when I dug down with my fingertips I pulled out a soggy cardboard box. Even before I brushed the mud from the face of it, I knew what it was—a pack of cigarettes.

I rubbed the box tenderly against the front of my hoodie then held it up to the last remnants of twilight.

"Lucky Strike?" I said.

Suddenly the crickets went quiet, and I got that strange shiver again. I looked around, but there was no one there. I looked back to the cigarette box.

The label looked old—like James Dean, Marilyn Monroe old—but the box was still in good condition, as if it had just been buried there the day before, and when I opened it, it was half-empty.

I pulled one of the cigarettes out.

The bottom tip of it was soggy, but the thing was fragrant—kind of rustic and sweet—and on the other end, I could swear I saw red lipstick that looked so dark in the twilight that it was almost black.

Without thinking, I brought the cigarette to my mouth. I set the end of it between my lips and let it hang limply there for a moment. The rustic smell set my senses on edge. I leaned forward, hugging my knees. I inhaled and exhaled, pretending to puff out smoke rings like I had seen so many actors do in the movies.

"You cruisin' for a bruisin', sweetheart?"

I turned, startled to see a young woman behind me, a few feet off, just inside the tree line. She wore a leather jacket and high waisted pants, and her hair was done up in a halo of perfect platinum curls. I knew she wasn't a fellow camper. I'd never seen someone like *her* before.

The cigarette fell from my mouth.

"Cat got your tongue? Whatcha doin' with my cigs?"

"I'm—I didn't—"

She was little more than a shadow, but I could see her dark eyeliner and dark red lipstick. She crossed her arms and looked over my head, tipping her head with a cocky sort of smirk.

"If I was you, I'd put an egg in your shoe and beat it."

"Wha—?"

I turned just in time to see Madison and her minions step onto the lakeshore, their flashlights flicking on all at once. Startled, I raised one hand to the lights and with the other I tucked the cigarettes into my back pocket.

"What do we have here?" Madison said. "A dirty little dyke?"

"Madison, hey—I don't want any trouble," I said, scrambling to my feet.

"You know where dykes belong?"

"Madison, wait—" I said.

"Under the water."

The other girls pushed toward me, driving me toward the water's edge. I searched for the strange girl I had seen before.

"Help!" I cried.

But she was already gone, and there was no way I was getting around Madison's gang on my own. With no other choice, I dived into water with the hopes of swimming to the dock on the other side. But no sooner had I taken a stroke or two did I feel their hands on my ankles, pulling me down.

I came up for air once but then they were on my back, all four of them. I kicked and punched and struggled against them, but my clothes were heavy and my limbs clumsy. Even with my eyes open I couldn't see through the murky water.

At first, I heard them chanting and laughing, but soon that faded away and the sound of my own heart took over. My lungs burned with the need to breathe. I reached a desperate hand out. I clawed at my attackers. I grabbed hold of someone's hair and pulled as hard as I could. A flashlight fell into the water, and like ghostly fingers, the lake weeds below reached up for me, ready to pull me further down into their darkness.

I felt a final, sudden push—someone's hands around my neck, squeezing, squeezing. I clawed and kicked, but it was no use. I thought distantly that I heard Madison screaming. I thought distantly that she had finally done it, had finally gone too far. But then her hands were gone, and I was left to float alone.

The flashlight flickered out, and with my eyes open and my lungs burning, I thought I saw the sliver of moon broken up into a million pieces above me until it looked like fireflies floating just over the water.

I can't say how long I floated in those still, dark waters.

But then I rose up to the surface with a start, coughing in desperation and relief. I looked to shore. I saw nothing, not even the hint of a flashlight. I heard nothing except the sound of crickets. And when I looked up at the sky, the moon was just the moon.

Cold and startled, I hugged myself as I waded to shore.

Silence.

I trudged into the woods, but the night was darker than I'd expected, and my mind was panicked and unclear. I found myself moving in circles, always coming back out to the shore when I should have arrived at the campgrounds.

I leaned heavily against a tree, took a deep breath, and told myself to wait for my eyes to adjust to the darkness.

But then I heard something—the sound of voices. They were girls' voices, happy and lilting with laughter.

I froze, thinking at first that it was Madison returning with her gang.

But the more I listened the more I was convinced that it wasn't her. The laughs were too hearty and the rhythm of speech was something different, all at once more delicate and deep. And mixed in with the voices, was a tinny song filled with harmonies, like a barbershop quartet on an oldies radio show.

"Hello?" I called out.

More laughter, more music.

I took a step toward the sound and then another. I scrambled up the side of a gently rising hill, and when I got to the top I saw the light in the distance; it came from an open window, and the window belonged to an old cabin that I'd never seen before.

The music was louder from there and the voices more clear. I still saw nothing.

"Read 'em and weep!" a girl shouted, her voice deep and husky.

I heard a smack of hands on a table, followed by a collective groan of disapproval and chairs pushed back in annoyance.

"Aw, come on, ladies, don't get frosted! I won it fair and square."

Without thinking, I found myself tiptoeing toward the open window.

"You won it, all right," a second girl replied, "but I ain't so sure it was fair, or square . . ."

I heard the poker chips scratch across the table. I stepped closer.

"Is that so? Then why don't you clue me in?"

"All right, sure. All I'm saying is you've won three hands in a row, and nearly all of our Lucky's. That's pretty good for someone who's never played before."

I stepped closer still.

"What can I say? Beginner's luck!"

Another smack against the table followed by a tense silence, the threat of which was only softened by the crooning of the voice on the radio.

"Or," the second girl said slowly, "someone's been lighting up the tilt sign from the start."

I slipped around the trunk of a tree and peeked inside the window just in time to catch sight of two girls, one facing my way and one with her back to me; one with a tight black pony tail and the other with a halo of platinum blonde curls.

The girl from the woods! I thought.

She had the same hair, the same leather jacket, the same attitude. She slouched back, reached into her pocket, and pulled out a pack of cigarettes.

"Look, Dolly, the last thing I want is to rattle anyone's cage," she said, placing a cigarette in her mouth. "Let's just call it a night, huh? I'll take what I've earned and beat it. No harm, no foul."

She pulled out a lighter and raised it cooly to her mouth, but she never lit the thing. No, she never even stood a chance.

BAM! CRASH!

Dolly shoved the table aside in a fit of rage, sending the cards fluttering into the air. The chips hit the wall and everyone scrambled. The blonde backed toward the window, but the other girls grabbed her, locking her arms behind her back and exposing her belly to Dolly's pocketknife.

I could not move. I could not look away.

I watched as Dolly flipped the knife in her hand—once, then twice.

"Come on, Dolly," the blonde grunted. "You know you don't want to do this—not over a bunch of cigarettes."

"No, Rosie—That's your name, isn't it?" Dolly said, moving closer. "What I *do* know is that you must think that I'm unborn or something."

"What're you talkin' about?"

"Do you think I'd let a paper shaker with a fancy nest come in here and steal my stash? Who sent you?"

"No one."

"Good," Dolly said with a smirk, "then no one'll miss you when you're gone."

BOOM! POW!

Dolly punched the knife twice and fast against Rosie's stomach, sending her lurching forward. She would have fallen, I'm sure of it, if it weren't for the girls holding her up. Dolly smiled and wiped at her own cheek before letting the knife fly again, and again, and again.

I closed my eyes, but I could not close my ears.

THUMP! THUMP! THUMP!

Dolly didn't seem to let up, but instead became more frantic in her attacks. Rosie cried out, but someone muffled her mouth. My last thought before I turned to run was of her red lipstick, of the way it must be smeared and smudged now.

I tore off then, running straight back in the direction I'd come from. I found my way to a footpath and followed it until I came to a large open clearing. I recognized the large oak tree and the shape of the mountain on the horizon.

This is it! I thought, breathless. *It's supposed to be here!*

But there was nothing there—no cabins, no cars, no campfire. There were no counselors to warn, not about Madison or the girl in the woods.

"Hello?" I shouted. "Help! Anyone?"

My voice echoed through the clearing, sending up a flock of birds that I heard more than I saw. I rubbed at my eyes. I was alone.

I fell to my knees, out of breath and confused. I leaned back and looked up. The stars looked the same, but the moon was full and low, when only moments before it had been a sliver set high in the sky.

"No," I whispered to myself. "No! I must be dreaming. I must be back at the lake. I'm still dreaming. None of this is—"

"Well, now," came a voice behind me. "Ain't that a bite?"

I jumped up. I spun around, horrified to see the girl with the golden curls. She stood with her hands in her pockets and her head tilted to the side. Totally relaxed, she regarded me with a smile, like she saw something both amusing and attractive.

"Don't say I didn't warn you," she said.

Rosie, I thought. *But you're dead.*

"Warn me about what?" I said, backing away.

I looked her up and down, searching for signs of violence, signs of blood. Her shirt was clean and white and it glowed in the moonlight.

"About your little scooch."

"My little what?"

Maybe it wasn't her after all, I thought. *Maybe it was another girl back in the cabin.*

"Your little scooch?" she repeated. "Your friend? The girl who jumped you at the lake? Am I speaking French here?"

"Oh . . ." I said, relaxing a bit. I looked around the clearing. "She's not my friend. And she's gone now. I mean, it's all gone—Something's not right. You should run! You should get far away from here!"

Dizzy and scared, I rubbed at my eyes.

"Don't think I haven't tried," she said. "Hey, you still got my smokes on you?"

Her question caught me off guard.

I reached for my back pocket. I pulled the pack out. It was completely dry in my hand, along with the cigarettes inside it. Astonished, I held them out to her.

"Here," I said. "Just take them and leave me alone."

Her eyes lit up as she reached for the box. "You don't know *how long* I've been looking for these."

When our hands touched, I felt a chill right up my spine. Her skin was surprisingly warm.

"Who are you?"

"What do you mean?" she said as she lit up.

"Back at the cabin? I saw you with those other girls. I saw you—"

She looked up, her expression stoic and unreadable. Then she puffed out a cloud of smoke and extended the open box to me. "Want one?"

"No," I said, hugging myself.

She shrugged and tucked the box into her jacket. For a moment she was quiet with her eyes closed and her head tilted back. The wind picked up and blew through her curls, but she didn't seem to notice. She took another puff, smiling as she exhaled. Then she turned her eyes to me.

"Look," I started, "something weird is going on and I should get back to camp, but—"

"But you don't know where it is? Can't seem to find it anywhere?"

I thought for a moment that her skin glowed like the moon. I thought that I could see right through her, but when I looked into her eyes, she was solid. I'd touched her after all. I'd brushed fingers with her. I knew that her skin was warm, just like mine.

I felt another chill.

"Yeah," I said. "Yeah . . . something like that."

"Well, maybe I can help you out with that—if you help me out first, that is."

"Help you with what?"

"I've been looking for something, and I think you can help me find it."

In contrast to her platinum curls, her eyes were dark brown and calculating. To be honest, I still wasn't sure I could trust her.

"What is it?" I said, hugging myself again.

"Just somethin' I lost a long time ago, probably over where you found these cigs. Say, where did you find them, anyhow?"

"Over by the lake, but I can't seem to find my way back there—something weird is going on. Everything is so confusing!"

"Well, don't go blowin' a gasket. I know where the lake is. Just follow me."

I did follow her. She walked and puffed, and walked and puffed, moving through the dark woods with a quiet sort of determination while I struggled to keep up. If our feet weren't taking us in circles, my mind was. I was unable to solve the equation of the present moment, unable to add together the moments that led up to me following behind a ghost of girl while she puffed on a sixty-year-old cigarette and whispered to herself about a secret stash.

And then the strangest thing happened—the fireflies.

They rose up from the forest floor, only a few bugs at first, but then there were hundreds, maybe thousands of them. I slowed to a stop and stared.

"Don't get distracted, sweetheart!" she called back. "We're nearly there."

"But the fireflies—"

"They'll only lead you further into the forest!" she called out. "Trust me."

I tried to trust her. I really did. I tried to take a step forward, to continue along the path, but then a firefly buzzed right before me. I reached a hand out, and the little thing nearly landed on my finger before drifting away. It seemed to beckon me to follow it.

And it was so beautiful that I did follow it.

I forgot about the girl with her leather jacket and her red lipstick, though only a moment before I had thought she was the most beautiful girl I'd ever seen.

No, at that moment, nothing was as beautiful as the little firefly. I followed it deeper into the woods, and as it drew closer to the other fireflies, they merged together, surrounding me in a wall of beautiful buzzing light. I felt them all around me, so many that I could not distinguish one from the other, nor could I see the forest beyond them, nor could I see the darkness of the night. I saw only light—warm and pulsing light.

I took another step forward, but then . . .

"You got smog in the noggin'?"

She jerked me backward by the elbow. I fell flat on my ass in the dirt as the little bugs scattered.

"What the hell?" I shouted, confused and angry. "Why didn't you just let me go?"

"We've got work to do. You made a promise, remember?"

I did remember.

"But they are so beautiful!" I said, stamping my heel in the mud like a child.

"Look, sweetheart, I don't know if you've quite figured it all out yet, but your friends aren't gone, and the campground isn't gone, either. It's you! *You're* the one that's gone—maybe just barely—maybe you have a chance to get back. But if you follow those damn bugs, you'll sure as hell never get home."

I watched as she spoke. I watched as the fireflies faded out. I watched as the blood soaked through the white cotton of her t-shirt, and her warm brown eyes became sunken and cold. I watched as her skin grew coarse and her hair grew white, and finally, the cigarette that she brought to her lips faded to ash in an instant and blew away on the wind.

She's dead, I thought.

But then she scowled and snapped her fingers in front of my face.

"Hey!" she shouted.

I blinked and she was back to her young self.

"Get up! I still need you," she said. "What did you just see?"

"I—uh . . . I . . . I don't know."

She grabbed my hands and lifted me to my feet.

That's when we both looked down. That's when we saw my clothes were soaked through and my skin was wrinkled and blue. Fat drops of murky water dripped from my sleeves onto the forest floor. I opened my mouth to speak, but all I could taste was mud. I gagged.

I'm drowning! I thought. *I'm still drowning!*

She must have seen the panic in my eyes because she lifted me up and pulled my arm over her shoulder.

"We're running out of time," she grunted. "Come on!"

She led me through the woods, never letting go of my hand. I stumbled over my water-logged shoes, and I choked on mouthfuls of mud, but she never let go. I fell twice and each time she lifted me up.

"Don't give up!" she said the first time.

"No," I choked back. "No. I can't breathe. Just leave me!"

"You still have lots to live for!" she said the second time.

My knees buckled beneath me, and we both fell forward. She reached for my face. She pulled me close to her, but I could barely see her through the watery facade of my own tears. I saw her mouth move but her words were muffled and unclear.

"You promised," I think she shouted.

I saw the fireflies gathering behind her—and growing brighter by the moment—as she pulled me close by my collar and then . . .

She kissed me.

Like being pulled from icy waters, I was both shocked and relieved.

"Please," she said, her voice quivering as her lips hovered just over mine. "Please, you don't know how long I've been waiting—how long I've been searching! I need your help. Don't you understand? I need you! Otherwise, I'll never know why they did this to me."

I heard her, but still I could not speak.

"I won't let you break your promise," she said, and she kissed me again.

Suddenly her breath was my breath; warm and alive. Suddenly her heartbeat was my heartbeat; determined and steady. I felt her warmth spread through my body, dancing across my skin like lightning.

And when she pulled away, I gasped, finally able to breathe. She smiled and in her eyes I saw a million refractions of the moon. But then she lifted me up onto my feet.

"Sorry, sweetheart," she said, "no time for dawdling."

And we were off again, hobbling together through the woods.

"Where are they?" she said when we came out to the lake shore. "Where are the cigarettes?"

"Over here!"

It took all of my strength to crawl out into the mud. She followed close behind, and in a moment of frantic digging, our fingers struck the top of something. We dragged the thing out. It was an old metal lunch box with a high rounded lid. Inside were stacks and stacks of Lucky Strikes, which she threw aside in search of something else. But when she got to the bottom of the lunch box there was nothing.

"It doesn't add up," she said. "There's no way they got so salty over a couple of cigarettes. All of this? Over a couple of cigarettes?"

Quiet, she stared down at the empty lunch box for a long time. Then she threw it across the shore, letting out a frustrated cry before slumping down into the mud and hanging her head in her hands.

I wasn't sure what she'd been looking for, but I was positive she hadn't found it. I reached a hand out. I touched the sleeve of her leather jacket even as I struggled to catch my breath.

"Sometimes," I started, "sometimes people are just monsters."

"Like Madison?" she said, looking up.

My ears grew hot at the mention of the name. I pulled my hand away, feeling suddenly exposed.

How much does she know? I wondered.

"Yeah," I said. "Like Madison."

"What are you going to do about her?" she said, tentatively.

"I don't know."

"I'd get rid of her," she said, punching the palm of her own hand with a tight fist. *Smack!* "Before she gets rid of you."

"I don't know if I can do anything like that."

"You're right," she said. "You're not the type."

"Maybe I should just stay here with you."

"No way I'm going to let that happen, sweetheart. Besides, I'm not going to be here much longer myself. I've got a date with the fireflies."

We both turned to see the little bugs gathering just inside the tree line. Even then, their light was so entrancing that I found myself leaning toward them.

"Oh no, not again."

She reached for my arm, but when that didn't work, she grabbed my face with both hands, pulling me close until all I could see were her brown eyes, and within them a lifetime of hope.

"Do you need another reminder?" she asked.

"A reminder of what?"

She leaned closer and smiled, brushing her thumb across my cheek, her brows furrowed in a sad sort of nostalgia.

"Of something to live for . . ."

Then she kissed me again, and a red, hot blush ran right over me, flushing my whole body with heat. I turned away from her. I reached for a pack of cigarettes. I turned it over in my hands, if only to have something to do.

"Um . . . I'm sorry you didn't find what you were looking for," I stuttered, "but I should probably get going. Can I take one of these with me?"

"Sure, why not?" she said with a shrug.

Unable to look her in the eye, unable to say goodbye, I opened the box and looked inside. It was packed tight with cigarettes. I lifted it to my nose and took a deep breath, anticipating the rustic, sweet smell of tobacco. But that's not what I smelled at all. What I smelled was something dank . . . sour . . . herbal.

"These smell weird," I said.

"What do you mean?"

She yanked the box from my hands, put it to her nose, and took a deep breath. Then, with a light in her eyes, she ripped the cigarettes from the box, fumbling until she had one in her hands. She ripped it open, scattering the innards across the mud.

"I knew it!" she shouted. She leaped over me, grabbing up every box. "Full of Mary Jane, every last one of 'em!"

She grabbed me up into a hug, laughing into my ear.

"I knew you'd bring me luck," she said. "You should have been there with me that night! I could've used a little luck then."

I smiled and brought another box to my nose, taking another sniff.

"Drugs? So that's why they—?" I said, but I couldn't bring myself to finish the sentence.

"God," she whispered, suddenly still next to me. "I walked right into that one, didn't I? I was such an arrogant, stupid fool."

"Well, at least they had a reason. Madison never had a reason to do what she did."

She looked at me then, her expression serious and strange. "No way, sweetheart. No one ever has a good enough reason. You hear me? Just because these are filled with dope instead of tobacco, that don't make anything fair. A monster is a monster, no matter what."

She was right.

"But what's done is done," she said, setting the cigarettes into the lunch box and closing the lid.

I stood up, too, and in the early morning light, I saw my body, floating up on the shore. I was both horrified and relieved to see myself, facedown, gently drifting until I was nudged up against the mud. I stood up, suddenly afraid.

"It's too late!" I cried. "I'm already dead!"

"Not dead," she said. "But dying. If I was you, I'd put an egg in my shoe and beat it. I didn't kiss you for nothin'."

"How do I—?"

"Just get back to your body before it's too late."

"And what about you?"

She turned toward the woods. The horde of fireflies was gathering behind her. She looked over her shoulder and thought for a moment.

"Don't worry about me," she said, hefting the lunch box up between her waist and the crook of her elbow. "I've got places to be, people to see."

The fireflies grew brighter and brighter behind her, lighting up the trees of the forest, lighting up the halo of her curls.

"Hurry up!" she shouted. "You've got plenty to live for."

She tapped on the lunch box before disappearing into a swarm of fireflies, their amber light so bright that I raised my hands to it.

But then the light was gone, and all was dark and cold and silent.

I turned back to shore and as soon as I saw my body . . .

I awoke with a gasp!

My lungs burned with the desire to live. I crawled to shore, heaving and heaving, evacuating my insides of the icy water I'd swallowed. And when I could not heave anymore, I laid absolutely still in the mud as the sun slowly rose overhead, my mind only half-conscious of my surroundings.

What finally roused me were the sounds of shouts and cries not far off.

I have to get up, I told myself. *I have to tell someone about Madison.*

But my body simply would not move. The water lapped gently around me and for a moment I thought it might be a peaceful way to go, but then I heard a voice, as snarky as it was sweet.

I didn't kiss you for nothin'.

I smiled at the thought, gathered my strength and stood up. I made my way slowly through the woods, and when I came to the clearing, I was relieved to see the campground, with its cabins and cars and camp circle. I was so happy to see the campers and the counselors, in fact, that at first I didn't notice how they milled around anxiously, whispering and pointing toward the front drive.

That's when I saw the police cars.

Oh my god! I thought. *I'm dead! I'm really dead!*

"Hey!" I shouted, running toward the closest campers. "I'm not dead! I'm right here!"

"Shh! What are you shouting about?" one girl said.

"Wait, you can see me?"

"Of course we can. Now, hush! They're bringing her out any second."

I followed their line of sight, looking across the campground to a cabin on the far side.

"Bringing who out?" I asked.

"Madison Queen," she said. "Apparently, she's like a drug dealer or something."

"What—?"

"Wait, here they come!"

We watched as two policemen led Madison out of the cabin by the elbow, her hands in cuffs behind her back. A third policeman followed behind, and tucked between his hip and his elbow was an old metal lunch box. He opened the lunch box and pulled out a pack of Lucky Strikes that looked old—like James Dean, Marilyn Monroe old.

Madison cried, shaking her head and screaming, but they led her to the police car anyway, and once the door was shut behind her, we didn't hear from her anymore.

"Well, well," I whispered to myself, "ain't that a bite?"

~

L.K. Early is an elementary school teacher who lives in North Hollywood, California. She has a degree in Media Arts from Emerson College in Boston. She spent the majority of her twenties living and teaching ESL in Seoul, South Korea. While there, her interest in the supernatural was bolstered in 2010 when she received a message from a childhood friend, shortly after learning of his death. Since then, she has listened eagerly to anyone and everyone who is willing to share their own stories about the beyond.

Black Hole
Halee Kirkwood

IMAGINE YOUR TEETH falling out. This summer, a girl will make you pregnant. Dream of your teeth's enamel browning like an apple set out in the sun, half-bitten. Your body no longer yours, but food for a thing.

You were so hard, for so long, your muscles sharp and shining and full of music when ground against the fit blades of the sun. Wield a machete in your hands, Northwoods lumberjack, heap brush and burdock at her feet while she sips a rose lemonade. Her summer dress, damp black cotton. Laugh at all that medicine and nobody sick. Light a bonfire. Hold her hand during the blood tests, hold her hand every morning she swallows her pills. See the femininity in the almond-slice of her eyes as you let her rock into you when you're too tired to push into her. Let what's left of her milk slide into you and begin to boil in the oven of your womb.

Make an appointment. Unmake paperclips as you imagine yourself softening, all of your hard-won strength relocating to your middle, feel the suck of the thing drain you. All of the medicine left at her feet, chars in the wind. Daydream yourself impossible, a slowly exploding red giant on *Oprah*, on *The View*, most definitely on the *Maury Povich Show*. For solace, daydream yourself the secret envy of nuns. Stay away from your axes and knives, from the verdant woodland that grants you life and sustenance.

She will crunch handfuls of granola on the drive to Minneapolis. Argue the merits of Taco Bell, bite aggressive half-moons into the burrito's vulnerable tortilla. Eat four burritos. Slurp Mountain Dew. Spot bunny rabbits and lollipops in the too-bright clouds stalking the passing farmland. Count the accumulating billboards, giant paper babies rising into the sky, swaddled in miniature motorcycle jackets, swaddled in bubbles and plastic ducks, swaddled in guilt. Note how they are branded with the x-ray silhouettes of paper mothers with long hair and soft bellies. Note it as a smoldering stamp of authenticity. Feel the thing roil inside of you like it already knows the orange bio-hazard box like home, haunts the orange box like a home, throw up in the car because you'd hate to ask her to pull over, hate to admit fear.

Hold her hand in the elevator. Pretend not to be mad that she took one of the pamphlets tossed like confetti by a wide-eyed man in front of the clinic, do not call her stupid or clueless when she responds "thank you" when he says he can offer help. She's just trying to help. Hold her hand at the secretary's window. Stifle a laugh when the woman asks if you two are sisters. Correct the secretary when she asks if it is your lover who is here for the procedure. Refuse the urge to look her in the eye and introduce yourself as the holy Madonna. As the mother of God. The Sapphic immaculate.

Cast your eyes downward while the ghost of who she never was comes back to haunt her. Father. Father. Father. Father of the child, with long tawny hair and eyelashes that curl up to meet her arched brow and wool skirts and cotton dresses and pretty little feet. A ghost who lives in paperwork, in a single letter. She does not cry. She is stronger than you.

When it is time, and you shiver, and you dilate, remember your body. While the cold metal rod is jammed like an unwound snake into your cunt remember the easy twist of an un-encumbered abdomen, remember yourself full of only yourself and not as a walking grave for a thing you had never even asked for but, even still, desperately want, a thing that should be in her and not you.

Do not, whatever you do, do not feel your skin and muscles and vaginal viscera and heart slide away from you like careless yolks from egg whites as the machine whirs to life and the thing cries and cries and you do not cry because that is a thing your body does not do, convince yourself that crying is a thing your body does not do.

And this is when it happens, the ghosting of your strength, when she wipes the sweat from your forehead while you lie helpless on the butcher-papered bed, and you say that this should all have been reversed, that you and her were born with the same hearts in the wrong bodies and, miraculously, it happens when you manage to notice how nice her lipstick looks today. Her face is pained, but she doesn't cry. Envy her knowledge, her ability to not take a body's mistakes too personally. Squeeze her hand tight.

Resolve, even as she pats your hair back and says that she loves, loves, loves you, resolve to pack her into a tidy little spaceship and ejaculate her far to the other side of the universe, where she won't be stretched like spaghetti in the vacuum of your body when finally the heat of your heart cools and transpires into a black hole. Two black holes—the one you are becoming, and the one that has nestled a vacant home inside of you, the aching, arthritic absence of the hungry, hungry thing.

You will know it's for the best. You will come down, back inside of yourself. You will write letters to her, cordial and well-wishing, hoping that she sips rose lemonade for someone else. You will miss her for forever, but you will be alone with your body, with your muscles. You will lift and chop and burn many things. But each time you move, you will feel the thing pulse with you, like a faint puff of air in your veins. And you will remember the near unmaking of your body for love. You will learn, in a cold white room, that it is better to be haunted by someone else than to be haunted by yourself.

~

Halee Kirkwood is a recent graduate of Northland College and a soon-to-be MFA candidate at Hamline University. When not babysitting books at the local public library, Halee can be found editing *Aqueous Magazine*, a free Lake Superior region literary and performing arts publication.

memories wicked little garden
Jamie Sage Cotton

white lies on cold lips
heaven howls
at the shadow of a corpse
and the memory of it falling
heaven howls
a tourniquet unneeded
and the memory of it falling
like ragged bandaged madness and
a tourniquet unneeded
sorrow fermenting in jars
like ragged bandaged madness and
the bleeding skin of a city
sorrow fermenting in jars
revealing
the bleeding skin of a city
where Medusa hoists her skirt
revealing
a handsome bed of deception
where Medusa hoists her skirt
singing of marriage and murderous things
a handsome bed of deception
the fangs of fear gnawing at my belly
singing of marriage and murderous things
sh, she says, sh
the fangs of fear gnawing at my belly
and the shadow of a finger to a mouth
sh, she says, sh
white lies on cold, cold lips

the shadow of a finger to a mouth
but seeing is not the same as hearing
white lies on cold, cold lips
and I told them I didn't see anything
but seeing is not the same as hearing
and I didn't know when I heard him begging
and I told them I didn't see anything
that he was begging for his life
and I didn't know when I heard him begging
while I kept my head down
that he was begging for his life
I was scared
while I kept my head down
I saw a shadow fall
I was scared
when they came to ask what I had seen
I saw a shadow fall
and I knew what could happen to pretty young girls
   in strange foreign countries
when they came to ask me what I had seen
I told them nothing woke me
I knew what could happen to pretty young girls
   in strange foreign countries
I knew I had to leave so
I told them nothing woke me
I did not tell them I was already awake
I knew I had to leave so
I lied
I did not tell them I was already awake
I lied
I lied
now I wake with a ghost gun in my mute mouth
I lied
and the shadow of a corpse

now I wake with a ghost gun in my mute mouth
the fags of fear gnawing at my belly
and the shadow of a corpse
as my bedfellow
the fags of fear gnawing at my belly
I wake and find
as my bedfellow
white lies on cold lips
I wake and find
a stranger whispering
white lies on cold lips
sh, she says, sh
a stranger whispering
and holding a strange unnameable fruit
sh, she says, sh
bite, chew, swallow—it won't hurt you anymore

~

Jamie Sage Cotton is a freelance writer, performance artists and filmmaker living in San Francisco, California with her partner their two dogs, two cats, a gecko, and twenty-one chickens. She has traveled and performed with Karen Horowitz's production of *Girl Meets Girl* and with her one-woman show "My Mother's Hand and other things that burn." Locally she has performed with The Queer Girl Theatre Project and is completing her first short film "Black Sheep."

They Come In Through the Walls
Bonnie Jo Stufflebeam

CLAIRE'S PAPA DOESN'T know her anymore. When they sit for dinner, he pushes his bowl of chili onto the floor. The bowl is plastic; after the first four times, she learned her lesson, but still it cracks as it hits the tile. The beans spread in a puddle beneath his feet.

"I won't eat your poison," he says.

"It's not poison, Papa. See." She eats a spoonful from her own bowl. "Aren't you hungry?"

"Not hungry enough."

Papa crosses his arms, surveys the rest of the table. It's a long table with twelve chairs, and before each chair a place is set. The phantoms will arrive soon, and when they do—Claire hopes—her father will eat. He always eats with the phantoms around.

In the kitchen the fluorescent light flickers. In the dining room, the flicker registers as a flash in the corner of Claire's eye, a minor annoyance but enough to drive you mad night after night. She needs to fix the light but has little time for household chores. Too much else to do: clean and cook and try to convince Papa to take his pills.

Claire goes into the kitchen to fill bowls for the phantoms. With the chessboard floor tiles below and the flashing light above, she feels like she's in a game, one of those video games maybe, the kind that comes with a warning: may cause seizures. She hurries, takes a bowl out for each place at the table and sets it atop the placemat. She fills the water glasses with wine and the wine glasses with water. She pulls the bread from the oven and covers the basket with a cloth, places it in the middle of the table. The phantoms won't eat the bread, but they'll devour the butter, leaving greasy stains all over her mother's white tablecloth. Claire places another bowl of chili before Papa. He doesn't touch it.

The phantoms come in through the walls, passing through the plaster and pink puffs of insulation as Claire imagines ghosts would. They look like silhouettes of people Claire may have met before, vaguely familiar in the outlines of their bodies. They take their places at the table. As they pull the chairs out, wood scrapes wood. Already there are rivulets dug in the floor. Claire will have to replace the floor if she ever wants to sell the house, after Papa goes. And the lights. Of course she'll have to fix those lights.

The phantoms eat with their mouths open, gray light pouring from behind their teeth, surprisingly white in their shadow faces. If Claire were to touch the light she imagines it would burn the skin. She never touches the phantoms.

They speak in deep voices, shaky as old men, and they speak often. Every night the same conversations.

"I was only twelve, and the man came to bring us our milk. He had a streak of black in his blonde hair, and I asked him what was the matter with his hair. He leered at me, always leering at me. I thought he was the devil," says one.

"Was he the devil?" asks another.

"Of course he wasn't. What are you, crazy?"

It's hard for Claire to place the voices to the mouths, for they talk even when their mouths are full of food. Chili drips down their chins. Outside the dogs bark at the door. The phantoms don't like dogs. They made that clear.

"What are those blasted noises?" Papa asks. "Can't a man eat his dinner in peace?"

Claire fixes another bowl and places it outside for them. They're Claire's dogs. They were her girlfriend's, before she left them and everything but her books and a brief note, another relic. Papa liked Claire's girlfriend more than he liked Claire. He used to call her Madeline, though her name was Anne. He liked her, he said, because she was funny. Claire has never been funny, and she suspects her father sees too much of him in her, that it confuses him. Anne was a blank slate, but too blank, it turned out; she absorbed too much. She couldn't take it, watching someone go like Papa. Claire never thought she should have to.

Now Claire lives alone with her father, and each night they dine with phantoms. Claire never asked them to be her guests. She isn't quite sure why they're there, in fact. She wants them to leave. Cooking for so many is expensive; it's hard enough when half of what her father eats ends up on the floor.

The truth is that the phantoms comfort him. When they're there, he seems less confused, less angry. He eats his dinner to the last bite. He laughs and tells stories. Makes it seem like the rest of the day was just a nightmare. Claire wants them to leave. She wants them to take her father with them.

It's a horrible thought she has more and more these days.

THE FIRST TIME the phantoms came for dinner there were fewer of them. Four months ago, right before Anne left. That night the fridge had nearly been empty, and Claire too tired after working her shift at the cemetery—she did ground maintenance there, in that silent paradise—to go to the store. She cooked what she could. Vermicelli spring rolls with peanut sauce, spaghetti with canned Alfredo, onion rolls two days past the expiration date. She cooked a lot of food without thinking; once she was in the hang of it, she didn't want to stop cooking. When she stopped, she would have to serve it. She would have to explain again to Papa that this was his home now, this was dinner. She cooked too much. So the phantoms came to eat it.

Walking into the dining room with Papa's plate in her hand, she saw the first one. It was only a vague shape then, a shapeless body and head made of black mist like car exhaust. But the elbows that seemed to rest on the tabletop were of a thicker consistency, nearly solid. Claire could make out an indistinct hum, like the low static of a television left on. Then she noticed there were more of them, three seats full, and her father seemed to be listening to something they were saying that only he could hear. She did what she could; she brought them plates.

After a couple of nights, their bodies began to turn as solid as their elbows, and Claire could hear their words like whispers. Unintelligible but full of inflection, hidden meanings she was sure. She tried harder. Every now and again she picked out a word: house, third, remember. Papa, it seemed, heard them as if they were part of him. Even when Claire heard nothing, he responded, and the phantoms bowed their heads and moved the holes that Claire came to call their mouths.

They were rude guests. They slurped their soup. Bits of food flew from their forks across the table. Claire cleaned up when they left. The phantoms always left through the walls as well, but they never went through the kitchen.

"It's the lights," Papa said. "You got to fix those damn lights."

ANNE HAD ALWAYS fixed the broken things. When the lights in Papa's room went out, Anne carried in the ladder from the garage and changed the bulbs. She changed the oil in Claire's car, bought a new hose for the washer. She knew how to do things like that. Claire had never been taught. She'd never been motivated to teach herself.

"I can't," Anne said the night before she left. "If we can't fix us, who will?"

They were in bed together, their clothes bunched at their feet, the blankets fallen to the floor. Their breath had steadied. The air in the room was stale in the absence of their sweat. That staleness had hung there, nameless, for weeks. It was overdue that Anne should mention it.

"I know what you'll say when I go. That I couldn't handle this whole situation, with your dad and all. But that's not it, Claire, and I think you know that."

"Right," Claire said, turning away. "Sure I do."

"If you won't talk to me, if you won't try. How can I help you if you won't talk to me about it?"

Anne tried to touch her, but she shrugged Anne off. It was this way no matter what. Claire wanted so badly to talk, but she swallowed it. It had to wait, until later, until later again, until later became months and the words she'd swallowed hardened like lead in her belly. There was no bringing them up again.

In the morning Anne packed the few things she kept there and left while Claire pretended to sleep. Once Claire heard the click of the front door, she wrapped her arms around her knees and rocked in bed.

The anger came later, though it was brief and soon replaced by the acquiescence of a caregiver, taking in events as they rushed forward to meet her. Swallowing them. Keeping them down with soda water and starch crackers, like the sick do.

"WHO IN THE hell is this?" Papa asked when he first met Anne. "What in the hell does she want?"

"This is Anne, Papa. She's my girlfriend," Claire said.

Anne shook his limp hand. He had always said that women should not shake hands.

"She looks like a man," Papa said.

Anne didn't look like a man. She had short hair, that was all, cut to her ears, black. Her skin was dark, her eyes brown. She wore black pants and a button-up purple blouse with a collar, a gray pea coat. Claire always thought she looked like she stepped out from a painting faded with age. It fit, because Anne was an artist of the digital era. She designed websites.

"It's nice to meet you, Mr. Pierce." Anne took her hand back but didn't look away from Papa. He was forced to smile.

"Are you here to bring me my lunch, Ms. Madeline?" he asked. "I'll take a tuna sandwich on rye."

In the kitchen Claire apologized. Her father wasn't always mean, she said, it was the disease. It brought something out that Claire had never seen before, only heard in a rumor from her mother, of her papa's temperament before she was born. A temperament that supposedly evaporated when he became a father. Claire's mother, before her death, always spoke of his transformation like it came from God. Claire didn't believe in God. Anne did. That was another reason Papa came to love her.

What he didn't tell Claire about Anne was that she reminded him of his own wife, three years deceased. She had the same laugh, the same way of moving through the room as if she'd been there all along. He knew this about her when they first met, but as time dragged on, he lost the chance to say it. He lost the memory as he'd lost his wife.

When she'd first gone, his wife, Claire's mother, Papa had not cried. Rather he felt a strange constriction in his chest, a tightness that kept him from holding Claire close. So he stayed in his chair, looking out the window, a book in his hand so he could claim he was busy if anyone tried to talk. Visitors. They came in droves, left casseroles on the kitchen counter, if Claire was there to let them in. If not, they left the steaming dishes on the front steps for Claire to bring in the next time she came to visit.

That was when the house had been his. It was not his any longer. He didn't know the pictures hung on the wall; he couldn't place the little striped bag in the bathroom or the light blue towel on the rack. The food in the fridge was foreign, exotic. All he wanted was a basket of fried pickles, but the woman in his house—she seemed so familiar—refused.

"Bad for your health," she said. "Here, Papa, eat this."

She called him that, and perhaps he was that to her, but she was not his daughter. He couldn't place her, but he knew this woman, so much older than the bits of Claire he could recall, did not belong to him.

It came and went. Then it went and never came back.

ONE NIGHT A phantom apologizes.

"I'm sorry. I should have been there better for you. I did wrong by you."

Claire has served a new kind of soup, French onion, which she hopes Papa will appreciate more than chili. She doesn't look up at the phantom; he's sitting at the far end of the table and is easy to ignore. But his words confuse her. Sometimes they do that, confuse her. They speak like her papa. They relay pieces of him he seems to have lost.

When she first noticed that they knew so much of the inside of his mind, she wished that they would give it all back. She's given up on hopes like that. Now the only wish is the one she's afraid and ashamed to admit. Take him, take him please. Take him with you.

"I should have told you it was going to be okay. All those words you probably needed to hear, I didn't give them to you," the phantom says.

Claire looks up at Papa. His expression is blank as he spoons French onion soup into his mouth. He doesn't look at her, though she sees him see her from the corner of his eye.

"Should've let you know I still loved you, even though you looked so much like her. Reminded me of her."

Finally Claire stands from the table, and without a word she walks to her bedroom. She needs a moment to breathe. It would have been a welcome apology from her father's throat. From a ghost of a memory, she never wanted to hear anything so personal. The words creep through her skin. She shivers. On the edge of her bed, she tries not to start shaking, but she has to grab hold of the nightstand to steady her hands.

There, on the stand, is one of the books Claire can never read again. Anne used to read it to her before bed. It's a book about the history of the movies, but it may as well have been a book of lullabies for how Anne's voice smoothed the words. Claire can't look at it. She ought to get rid of it, but she can't bear to touch it. In the DVD player, there's a movie Claire can't make herself remove.

Alone in the bedroom, Claire hears voices from the dining room as clear as if they were there with her. They could be coming through the vents, but she doubts that's the case. She lies across the bed and unbuttons her shirt, wriggles out of her jeans. The cotton sheets against her skin is soothing. The air from the fan blows down on her, though never will either feel as soothing as Anne's hands, or her mother's.

Eventually Claire will have to get up from the bed. She will have to go back into the dining room and clean up the mess. For now she will let the room take care of him. She will let the phantoms comfort him. She closes her eyes and thinks about her mother, the way she flipped her hair back to clear it from her face. Her white white teeth, the rare smile, less rare when she and Claire were alone.

Anne was something like her mother, but her smile was for everybody. It was what Claire liked most.

Claire rolls over face down on the pillows. They smell like fresh laundry. Claire's breath catches. They will never smell like Anne again. She's washed it away. It's a step she hadn't thought she'd taken, and the pressure building in her chest tells her it's a step she wasn't ready for. How could she have done that without noticing? She curls against the pillows and makes herself cry, for Anne, for her mother, her papa, her everyone.

THINGS CLAIRE CANNOT touch for fear of losing them:

    1. The CD she made for Anne but never gave her.
    2. The books, mostly on the bottom shelf, all gifts.
    3. Her mother's old silver-plated mirror and comb.
    4. The pillowcases she won't wash again.
    5. The recipes in the recipe box, written in her mother's hand, one in Anne's. Her father's scratchy instructions for a "secret tortilla soup." Food she can no longer eat.
    6. The dirty pair of underwear Anne forgot beneath the bed.
    7. The bandages Anne bought to bind the burn on Claire's hand from cooking.
    8. Her father's Christmas trinkets, still up from December in June.

9. Her father's photo album, full of blank spaces.
10. Her father's hand.

PAPA NEVER WAS one for apologies, for feelings. None of them were.

Here is Claire, the past: an open letter in her hand. She bounds into the kitchen, where her mother stands at the stove. The smell of fish frying, the greasy scent of hot oil, catches Claire at the threshold. She pauses only a moment before she waves the letter through the air.

"I got in!" she yells.

Her mother turns, smiles, turns back to the stove. "That's great, dear."

As if her excitement were a balloon suddenly popped, the air wheezes away. Claire stands with a letter in her hand, unsure. Tosses the letter on the table.

Despite her initial excitement, after a semester Claire drops out.

Instead she holds as many odd jobs as she can until she happens on the cemetery position. Claire's been there now for fifteen years. Without a home to call her own, the cemetery grounds become the place she most likes to be. There she can fix things. When the grass gets too long, she cuts it. When the flowers die, she replaces them. When she happens upon someone crying, she in no way feels obligated to comfort them. Her place is in the background of their lives, safe.

Being the center of Anne's life made her uncomfortable. Always she felt on edge, her limbs rigid, her back tight. Anne tried to massage the knots away, but it didn't work, because when Anne's hands left her skin, the knots returned. She didn't know how to explain this, to tell Anne it wasn't her fault.

Claire can't remember ever seeing her parents kiss. She can't remember them kissing her. Now, in her bedroom, she does not remember Anne's lips.

IT WASN'T A surprise when the doctor called Claire and told her she would have to find care for her father. Her father had been forgetting; it started when her mother was sick and worsened after the funeral. Little things. When Claire would call, he would tell her the same story in the course of thirty minutes. He forgot where he put his wallet. Claire became the caretaker of his credit cards, as he could no longer keep track of the payments. He wrote bad checks.

Then he forgot where he was. He asked for his mother, long passed. The first people he forgot were insignificant: actors, politicians, cousins who never visited. Then it was the post man, his nephew. Finally it was Claire, as the doctors had warned.

"Where's my little girl?" he would ask, and she would explain. She would explain again. At first it was temporary; it would, eventually, come back to him. "Claire," he'd say, squeezing her hand. "You're back. I sure do like it when you visit."

"Of course, Papa," Claire would say. "Don't worry, I won't stop visiting you."

The memory of her mother, on the other hand, was harder for him to lose. It seemed as if, though it too came and went, it was more often present. He remembered her, but her absence was something he couldn't explain to himself. He asked about her all the time back then.

These days he doesn't ask about her at all. Claire envies him his ignorance.

Claire didn't move in right away. At first she hired caregivers to stay with him 24/7. Then the money ran out, the savings dried up, the cards maxed out. Social security and Medicaid paid for only half the care, and Claire didn't make enough to pay the rest. She broke the lease on her apartment and moved back in.

Anne came along later, at Claire's yard sale. She'd cleaned out Papa's old things, antiques he let rot in the garage, a bicycle missing its tire, the clothes he no longer wore—these days he mostly donned his favorite blue robe and plaid pajamas. Anne wasn't really interested in the merchandise, but she bought the bike so she could talk to Claire. She arranged to pick it up later, when she wasn't on her way to the store. She lived in the neighborhood, she explained. Claire thought she talked too much, a trait she would learn to love.

Now she misses the voice. Silence fills the empty air. Except when the phantoms come and take it, and there is no comfort in their stolen words.

THE STORIES THE phantoms tell are familiar to Claire. Every night at dinner she feels nostalgic with each mouthful of chili, and it isn't the food, though that too comes from a memory of limbo years with a crockpot and three cans of beans. She likes the nostalgia of taste buds. What falls from the phantoms' mouths, she likes much less.

Papa told her some of the stories the phantoms have adopted, and her mother told her others. The rest are new to her, but they ring with her father's voice. She hates hearing her father's words from so many gray mouths. She hates not being able to look at him when she responds. He finds the phantoms entertaining; the stories are new to him.

The evening of the apology, once Claire returns to the dining room, she finds her father still there, his guests gone.

"It's time to go," he says.

"Okay," says Claire. She moves to help him, wraps her arm around his arm. "Let's go to bed now, Papa."

"No." He jerks his arm away. She thinks she knows what's coming next; he will throw a fit, tell her to leave him alone, tell her to take him where he belongs.

But he doesn't. Instead he looks at the wall, the spot from which the phantoms leave. Claire looks there as well. One of the phantoms is still on this side of the wall. It extends a gray arm. "Time to go."

Her papa pats the table. "Be right back," he says. Suddenly

Claire knows it's a lie. She can't explain how she knows it. Her father will go, and he won't come back.

She leads her father to the hand. The shadow consumes him, his arm, his shoulder. It pulls his body forward, and together he and the phantom walk through the wall. Through the plaster Claire hears her father's voice. "Those damn lights. Hope she remembers."

Once he's gone, Claire can't quite move. She stares at the spot where he stood. It was sudden, she thinks, more so than she thought it would be. She's not quite sure—she has to consider what has happened—if she's had time to build herself up to this. If she'll be able to get through this without anyone anymore to call hers. She wraps her arms around her chest. The room is cold. The dogs outside howl. She lets them in. There is some vague kind of comfort in their fur. They lick the smell of onion from her hand.

Once they've settled down, she goes into the kitchen, pours the soup into a plastic container, slides the container into the fridge. She rinses the dishes and loads the washer. Stands on the cabinet and tries to pull down the light cover. The side cracks in her hands, and a shard of glass crashes to the chessboard floor. Like a pawn, she thinks, too small to be significant. Back on the floor she moves the glass from square to square. Crumbs dig into the palms of her hands. One square at a time, she slides the glass to the edge of the kitchen, then over, into the dining room. She considers picking it up, throwing it away, but she doesn't. She crosses her legs where she is and waits to see if the light will stop flickering, if her father will after all come back.

AS FOR ANNE, there's a phone and a number. Claire still remembers, after all.

"The first order of business," Anne says once Claire lets her in, "is that light."

Claire has already thrown away the glass on the floor. She's already cooked a pan of tomatillo enchiladas for them to eat for dinner. The table she has set for two.

"Okay," Claire says.

It's really all that need be said.

~

Although Bonnie Jo Stufflebeam has tried, she has not thus far succeeded in walking through walls or cooking a meal without burning it. Her fiction has appeared in magazines such as *The Toast*, *PRISM International*, *Clarkesworld*, and *Hobart*. She holds an MFA in Creative Writing from the USM's Stonecoast program and curates the annual Art & Words Show in Fort Worth, Texas. You can visit her on Twitter @BonnieJoStuffle or at www.bonniejostufflebeam.com. She is represented by Ann Collette at Rees Literary for her first novel about a mother, a daughter, and a siren.

Angel of Light
Doreen Perrine

HERE I TRAIL the edges of land and sea, and I survive. Survive, not live. The words that crash through my barren spirit are no longer synonymous. Like shells crushed underfoot, perception is shattered across this meandering shoreline. A foaming necklace where water meets sand evokes the picture of pearls I once gave you. See how your memory haunts me? I cannot even stroll along the beach in peace.

I hardly sought you out, and hadn't my heart already been plundered? Yet you'd clapped my door knocker, a grotesque gargoyle to keep intruders at bay, with a thunderous clang. Clad in white, you emerged through mists of a howling storm—fitting backdrop for your phantom figure.

You told me your name, "Dee," and confessed your escape as the mistress of some aged nobleman. Since girlhood, imagination has been my tragic flaw, yet I could not—dared not—imagine your comely form in the arms of some wrinkled man. Six years your elder, I was swayed by your crisp, blue eyes and the strands of your honey brown hair, twisted by rain. Rainwater streamed from your frame like golden drops in the halo of my lantern's light, and I was too mesmerized to avert my eyes from you. Was it death or a phoenix-like hope to resurrect my tortured heart you brought? I welcomed both.

In the wake of heartbreak from a cruel lover who'd cast me aside, I should have reflected better. Like a widow grieving her lies, I'd collapsed on her doorstep after she had locked me out one rainy night. Unbeknownst to her husband and to me, she'd taken another lover—a drunken actress—to her bed. I fled their icy domain of the city, longing only to be forgotten and to forget by this sea.

A half year later and despite the gaping scar of that lesson, I suffered you to enter my home. Still I fretted: your lord and master might search for you. "Let him come," bold words amidst my brewing fears to endure the loss of love once more. "Should you wish to leave, by all means, go." I swept my arm in a dramatic display. "Meantime, we'll harbor in this fortress"—the crumbling ruins of my family's manor.

"None shall seek me," you murmured with downcast eyes that searched the ground for something or someone you might never find.

"Are you certain?" I asked with a gingerly pointed finger to lift your chin.

Beneath the shroud of a hood, you met my gaze with an orphaned look, and I couldn't distinguish your tears from rain. Your shiver beckoned me to lead the way up the staircase that wound with our creaky steps past cracked portraits of my ancestors. In the shifting glow of my lantern, their faces appeared to follow your motion with wary and wistful smiles.

We entered my bedchamber where I slid the velvet cloak from your fair shoulders. It crumpled in folds of white onto the stony floor, and, stark naked, you shivered more violently. Was it dampness or my watching you in the glimmer of light that shook your frail frame?

"I'm no stranger to keeping secrets," I said in a tender whisper as I dried your hair with the towel old Nessa, my one servant, had handed me from across the threshold. Ignoring the unspoken worry in her creased, gray brows, I bid her to leave. Alone, you might share your tale, but you barely sipped from the teacup I held to your speechless lips.

Nothing so much as your lamblike silence lured me to press your breasts, chilled from rain, against my chest, to kiss your mouth, and take you to my bed.

In the midst of our instant passion, you uttered one faint word, "Undying."

I hear it still, a hushed echo sealed within my chamber walls in the darkest depths of night. Now only the sea responds with endless laps of waves. I no longer answer you.

EACH NIGHT I sheltered you, I bolted the chamber so that Nessa, limp and hard of hearing, might leave us free to explore. "She was my nanny ages ago and might not approve." I chuckled as I nestled my cheek on your soft shoulder.

"She loves you like a mother," you said with a melancholy hush that lingered into silence.

We sprawled on a tattered Turkish rug before the yawning fireplace. With flames as fierce as my desire, firelight swathed our mingling flesh, and more than words, your tender blush, silken skin, searching fingers and tongue, spoke to me. Then, after that first night of bliss, my overwhelming lust plunged me headlong into love—the greatest curse of all.

How long did you stay? Memory evades rational thought with futile mockery. Why mock a brokenhearted fool with no more secrets to absolve? Was it a fortnight or a month? Or one more oblivious half year? I no longer recollect.

Like the crush of a cresting wave, our bliss had gotten washed away in mournful nights. You wept, first soundlessly, and then with throbbing sobs. Your body quaked, and I rocked you, often through the night, and, as my mother had once sung to me, a child in her arms, I lulled you into tranquil sleep. Torn with blind desire, I watched your dreaming face in wonder. What had that foul man done?

Given a poor inheritance and no need to wed, I live sheltered from the burden of marriage and motherhood. A fatherless daughter and husbandless woman, I linger, a last broken link to the chain of my heritage. The beauty of a dying dynasty is scant pressure to preserve lineage. Your origins humble and too vague, you must have been forced to please that beast against your will. Once, I'd declared amidst our lovemaking,

"There is no deeper passion like a woman for her kind." As though you wholeheartedly agreed, you returned a smile more beatific than the grandest of the portraits.

Yet our passion swiftly plummeted to a bitter death. Your hungry kisses, the warmth of your embraces, your echoing moans so that even my lazy dog barked at the sound, all abruptly ceased. You winced at my touch, and, to my horror and despair, your gentle eyes transformed into a familiar, icy blue.

You spewed venomous words in sudden fits of rage; you protested that I lied whenever I fervently swore, "I love you," even upon bended knees. I'd only taken you in to tarnish your virtue or to wrestle your forlorn spirit from your soul. You no longer spoke but to blame, and I began to yearn for our first tacit days.

Then with your face as dark and whirling as a riptide, you screamed utter nonsense. "You have abandoned me and our babe unto death!"

Naturally, I stood innocent of the heinous accusation—*What child? What abandonment?* And what point in defending myself? Someone hurt you, him, I surmised, the villain you saw reflected in my baffled gaze. And as though you passed a hand through my solid form, I faded to invisibility in your eyes.

Your tongue grew so callous I checked every word, and, in my spirit, retreated into solitude. The greenhouse of shattered glass and shriveled plants and wandering across the beach were my sole refuges. Any escape was better than your dredging up this wave of thwarted emotions. Alas, my torture had been the lashing tongue of the woman I'd escaped to forget. My sole demon after healing from that heartbreak, loneliness, I ought to have embraced and to have shut out your light.

Why didn't I padlock my door when you'd first knocked? Why not latch my shutters so that no more than moonlit shadows might disrupt my peace? Remote stars in a blackened sky present little danger of wishing on. I should not have dared to hope.

Ever since your disappearance, I leave the grasp on reality to braver souls. In between this rush and sweep of endless waves, my only thought is loss.

NOT UNTIL THE tenth anniversary of my mother's death, did I fully understand. I picked a bouquet of wildflowers and plodded with my ambling dog in the direction of the churchyard. I made my way, veiled by my floppy hat, up and across the meadow that trailed into the graveyard's timeworn path.

Lost in the shadow of the looming church, something held my steps, and I turned onto a weedy path. I was met by a marble angel that bore the names of a baron, his wife, and three sons. As I sidestepped the angel, whose wings were chipped along their tips, a sliver of white in a mound of brush caught my eye.

I waded through weeds to spy an eroded slab etched with a faint inscription. Furiously, I ripped up grass, and then I flopped, gasping, to my knees. I squinted to read: *D and Child. Died 1783*—a hundred years before!

The flowers' petals became a blurred shambles before my eyes as they seemed to drip from my limp fingers to the earth. My breath quickened in frenzy as I clutched my curls and my thumping chest. *What*, I wondered crazily, *drew me to this forgotten grave?* "Is this you?" I whispered through an achy sob that wended from my heart into my mouth.

The dog trotted, eyeing me with troubled glances as I stumbled home to find old Nessa.

She rubbed her chin with a pensive nod. "Mmm. In my childhood," her raspy voice echoed in the musty parlor, "I heard tell of a servant, a pretty orphan, turned mistress to the lecherous baron the moment she had come of age. They say she died giving birth to his bastard son."

Nessa cast a gaze as withered as her face toward the bow window that faced the sea, crimson in sunset. "His lady," she said, breaking my dumbstruck silence, "accused the poor creature of losing her virtue to another man. Yet everyone knew the truth of her swollen belly. The girl had come to the baron's household as virgin pure as driven snow." Nessa waved her bony fingers with a flourish. "Still, the lady tossed the girl, who could not conceal her birth pangs, into the stormy night."

Nessa's flare for melodramatic tales had always amused me. Until now.

"The baron, said to be as stone cold as the grave under which his mistress and child lie, commanded his butler, who pleaded to let the girl inside, to bolt the doors." Nessa clamped a bracing hand that seemed to drive the story into me. "Amidst the woman's wails and pounding on the door, man and wife sat down to supper."

I sharply bit my lip until I tasted blood, and, unable to move, burned my gaze into the fire.

"On stormy nights," Nessa wagged her tousled white head, "'tis said the young woman, whose name the villagers forgot, haunts these shores in the shroud of a white cloak." Her shriveled body hunched, Nessa stroked my sunken head.

"What did she seek?" The question seemed to numb my lips.

"I've heard tell she relives that deathly storm, seeking the one who will welcome her inside."

And the fool who will love her back to life?

"Child," Nessa said in a nearly inaudible whisper, "did you shelter her?"

Lightning split the blackened sky as shock tore through me. As though to bolster the fragments of my addled thoughts, I reached for Nessa's hand. My knuckles whitened with my grasp, and I slumped on my father's throne-like chair.

I couldn't think to speak.

AT TIMES I imagine I had dreamt you, a vision that shimmers in and through haunted memories. Other times, I believe that each night we lay, side-by-breathing-side, an angel had blessed my bed. *Angel of light or death?* I cannot say and neither do I care which. You are but a rotted corpse below a slab that bears one letter of your name. The shadow of a broken existence, now you sleep in peace. I don't.

Mementos torment me with hints of the tangible—a wooden ornament of kissing doves, a heart-shaped pillow embroidered with *D loves D*, the chalk slate from the dusty nursery. On it, you had written, *You amaze me!* How amazing could I be? You left me as mysteriously as you passed out of my world and onto the other side.

Throughout each nighttime storm, I watch the shoreline from my chamber window. My dog, his eyes drooped with a look of futile pity, keeps vigil over me. I dare not budge from my window seat where, other than frothy waves and the billow of clouds, nothing stirs in darkness. Yet I strain my eyes with hopeless hope to spot a solitary figure in a stark white cloak.

You no longer haunt this shore. Now I visit yours, instead of my own mother's grave, and the love that I unbolted my door too quickly to bestow, has wrought your final resting place. Precious little comfort as I walk this beach that never seems to end alone—a breathing phantom who forever mourns the loss of you.

~

Doreen Perrine's novels are published through Bedazzled Ink, and her stories have appeared in *The Copperfield Review*, *Lacuna*, *Raving Dove*, *Freya's Bower*, *Harrington Lesbian Literary Quarterly*, *Sinister Wisdom*, *Queer Collection*, and in the *Through the Hourglass* anthology of lesbian historical fiction. Doreen is a recent finalist for the Golden Crown Literary Society's Goldie Award and South Africa's *Bloody Parchment Literary Festival*, and the recipient of a PEN Writer's Relief Award. Doreen's plays have been performed throughout New York City, and, in her other life, she's an artist and teacher who calls herself a city hick in the Hudson Valley of New York. Her website address is: http://www.doreenperrine.com/

The Haint on Cryin Baby Bridge
Xequina Ma. Berber

YEAH, I'VE HEARD "Ode to Billy Joe." Who hasn't? How he jumped off a bridge and everybody discusses him over the black-eyed peas like something on TV It was a song by Bobby Gentry, created a big stir because it was so mysterious and symbolic, everyone wanted to know what it meant. That was obvious: nobody cared about a dumb hillbilly without enough sense not to kill hisself.

Weird thing is, that song came out just before someone I knew really did jump off a bridge. We were in seventh grade when we started doing stuff together. Don't know why Jimmy Jean, called J.J., took a shine to me. Maybe she could tell there was something different about me too. Knew it long before I did. She wore baseball caps long before it was cool, and taught me the proper names of bugs and trees. We'd catch snakes and turtles and go out to the swimming hole, but J.J. didn't ever go deep. She was afraid of the water on account of almost drowning when she was little.

Otherwise, J.J. was the bravest person I knew. She would fight boys bigger than her even if it meant she was going to get whupped. Once in the children's section at the library a man got his weenie out. Us kids were peeking and laughing, but J.J. got mad and went after him with a bat. He only got away because of this lame foot J.J. had from the way she was born.

We talked about all kinds of things. She explained the difference between plain old naked (like when you go skinny dipping), buck naked (you still have something on, like socks), bare-ass naked (every last thing off), and nude (how models get for artists, and it's not nasty). She told me how to get a baby, and we both took vows we'd never let a guy do that to us. That led to practice kissing—my idea, so we'd know how when we went on dates. J.J. always volunteered to be the boy. Kissing led to fooling around—J.J. starting it because she said that's what boys do next, only I wouldn't get p.g. with a girl.

People saw her go off that bridge, but they didn't see why. I knew. I was with her when it happened. It was summer, getting late. We were walking across the Telame Bridge, just hanging out, talking. About halfway across, these two hoodlums, about seventeen years old get on the bridge and start coming toward us. They hated J.J., were always calling her "dyke." I didn't know what that was, thought it had something to do with the geography of Holland. J.J. stayed away from them. She let it slip that they'd done something to her once, she wouldn't say what. Just that they'd tied her up first.

So J.J. sees them and says oh great. Of course we were near the middle of the bridge. We turn round and start walking back the other way, fast as J.J. could go, which wasn't very. You run, she told me. Don't wait for me. I looked back. I thought maybe those guys would be nice this time, they were smiling, not hurrying. I say, what about you? Do it! She yells, so I did, but once off the bridge I looked back to keep an eye on her. J.J. was getting closer to the side of the bridge. When they caught up with her Eli starts to grab J.J., but she twisted away from him and got to the very side of the bridge. I screamed NO when I saw what she was going to do, but she jumped, holding her knees, cannonballing like she seen me do, down into the dark water of the Telame.

We all stood staring at where she went down, me holding my breath like I was doing it for her. J.J. didn't come up. I scrambled down by the side of the river, looking all along the bushes and trees, screaming her name, but she was gone. You killed her! I screamed at those two idiot peckerwoods. We weren't goin to do nothing, Eli yelled back. Why'd she have to go and jump? They came off the bridge at me so I took off running. You better not go telling any lies on us, Cash yelled after me. We know where to find you.

Couple of kids fishing saw J.J. jump, pretty soon everyone knew what she done. Cash and Eli acted like they were heroes trying to stop her from jumping. Sheriff talked to me too, asked what I saw, if she'd been depressed, had she ever talked about killing herself. I thought that was like blaming her somehow. Yet I didn't tell what happened. I wasn't brave like J.J., I was scared of those two bullies. Then Sheriff said until we found the body, we couldn't even say she was dead.

Ma said Jimmie Jean wasn't too smart, going around looking like a boy, competing with them an everything. She drew attention to herself. You can't do that if you're "different." Did she think this was California? My brother said people like that should tiptoe, but carry a big stick with a nail in it. So you see this story is a lot like that song. That's why I couldn't listen to it again.

They dragged the river but never did find J.J. I figured she got stuck in some place deep under sunken trees and eaten by river animals. Just the sight of fried catfish could make me throw up. I stayed home moping till Ma made me go out with other friends. Mary Sue Parsons down the street was real nice to me, but it wasn't the same.

School started but I couldn't concentrate no more. I was stunned from watching my best friend drown and really mad at myself for being a coward. First I betrayed J.J. by leaving her, then by keeping quiet, even if it wouldn't have served a purpose. Eli and Cash actually *had* tried to keep her from jumping, and I didn't know what made J.J. want to keep away from them enough to make her jump into deep water.

On Halloween night I went with Mary Sue to chaperone her little sisters trick-or-treating. A full moon painted the houses and roads with a soft ghosty light. The smell of burning chimney smoke filled the air with the reminder of winter coming. After they got a bunch of candy the little girls asked can we go out to Cryin Baby Bridge. That's a nickname for the Telame. Story is a long time ago, someone left a baby there who wasn't found till after it was dead. People said when it was real quiet, you could hear it crying.

Mary Sue looked at me. I hadn't been back there since J.J. jumped, but I was gonna have to face it sometime or other, so we headed over. The houses got less and less the closer you got to the river. The black, leafless trees looked like long, skinny fingers scratching at the sky for mercy. The little girls were all excited and kind of scared about maybe hearing a ghost. They talked about Casper being a little boy ghost, and he was nice, so why wouldn't a baby ghost be?

When we got there, who should we see but those pudding-headed guys Cash and Eli, on the middle of the bridge, smoking. They sees us, that we're just four girls, especially me, the prize-winning chicken shit of the county, and Eli says hey let's beat up those kids and get their candy. Mary's sisters screamed and started running, but I couldn't move. I just stood there with my mouth falling open because I couldn't take my eyes off the other end of the bridge.

It just appeared out of the darkness, a girl, soaking wet, wearing a long, muddy T-shirt plastered with leaves. She had something, a fishnet I guess, tangled around her head, and through it you could see her eyes were big dark hollows and her mouth all bruised purple and bloody against her white face. She had pretty little cherub wings, and she was holding her hands clasped in front of her like she was praying. A sort of light came from her, especially around her head, like in the pictures of saints. Mary Sue screams it's Jimmy Jean! and Cash and Eli look back, and at first they just stood staring too. Cash says, what is it? Eli says it's just a kid in a damn costume, but he didn't sound so sure.

Then J.J.'s ghost started floating toward them, pointing at them standing there with their mouths gaping. She said in a whispery voice that seemed to seep into my ears and make all my tiny hairs stand on end The Devil told me he's waiting for you 'cause of the rotten lives you live!

It-it's a haint! yells Eli, and he grabs Cash by the jacket and they run screaming into the night like a pair of ambulances from the scene of a crime. Me, I ran toward her, calling J.J.! She was so real I thought she'd come back. But when I tried to throw my arms around her she broke up and disappeared. Nothing and no one was there.

When I got back Mary Sue was standing there brave as can be, her little sisters holding onto her dress with cartoon-big eyes. She held me while I cried. I hadn't cried over J.J. I thought if I did, I was admitting she was really gone.

None of us talked about what we seen. We just went home. I went straight to bed and cried and cried. After three days Ma brought in the root granny. She laid her warm hand on my forehead and looked in my eyes and said Girl, you've had a powerful fright. She sat there and prayed and blew tobacca on me with her corn pipe. That night I dreamed of J.J., laughing, happy as a honey bee.

Some months later Ma went to the city to shop and my brother was working. I was reading a book in the parlor. It was a breezy day, that warm kind of light wind that comes along and makes you glad for spring. Something like a shadow that wasn't, passed the front of the house. I don't know how else to describe it, because it wasn't dark. I looked out the window, but no one was there. Then I noticed something white on the floor by the door. It was an envelope made of the lightest paper, and when I picked it up I saw my name in J.J.'s loopy handwriting! The paper was delicate, probably weighed less than a paper stamp, which it didn't have. Instead it looked like it had a rubber stamp of an angel's wing, only the ink was gold. Inside was a piece of see-through paper. On it was written,

> I now your feeling gilty bout what hapended. You have no caus to, cut it out. You get here and wondr what was all that fear we had round dying. If you knew you could not wait to get here, and no one

> would have a life. Everyone needs a life so have a good one.
> Love you.
> Jimmy Jean
> PS even our old pets are here.

I ran outside and looked up at the sky, but all I saw was distant clouds. Then I felt something touch my cheek, and I was sure it was J.J. kissing me goodbye.

THE GHOST OF J.J. put the terror of hellfire into those two useless no counts. They stopped hanging out together. Eli suddenly found ambition and started working his family's farm. Cash studied his Bible and became a deacon at the Methodist church, eventually going to seminary. Neither ever said what caused their profound changes.

I think in her song, Miss Gentry was saying people need sympathy, no matter if they're just a dumb hillbilly or homosexual or colored or foreign, whatever. Without it you go over a bridge, or become a hateful hoodlum. As such, I forgave Cash and Eli for their part in taking J.J. away from me.

I hope Billie Joe and J.J. will keep each other company till I get there.

~

Xequina Maria Berber has been writing since third grade. She holds a Master's degree in English Literature and another in Women's Spirituality. She is of Mexican-American descent and the author of *Santora: The Good Daughter*, a novel loosely based on her strange life, and a children's book, *The Mermaid Girl*. She came out during early middlessence and now makes up for lost gay time through her creative endeavors—short stories, comic strips and paintings celebrating lesbian themes and personalities. She also rewrites songs to honor dyke culture, which are then performed for the community with her partner Rome. Xequina lives in Oakland and works as a school librarian.